The Diary

of

B. B. Bright,

Possible Princess

The Diary
of
B. B. Bright,
Possible Princess

Alice Randall
and
Caroline Randall Williams
Illustrations by Shadra Strickland

TURNER

Turner Publishing Company

200 4th Avenue North · Suite 950
Nashville, Tennessee 37219

445 Park Avenue · 9th Floor
New York, New York 10022

www.turnerpublishing.com

The Diary of B. B. Bright, Possible Princess

Cover design by Gina Binkley
Interior design by Glen Edelstein
Illustrations and artwork by Shadra Strickland

Library of Congress Cataloging-in-Publication Data

Randall, Alice.
  The diary of B.B. Bright, possible princess / Alice Randall [and] Caroline Randall Williams.
    p. cm.
  Summary: Held captive on an island, thirteen-year-old orphan Black Bee Bright must pass her Official Princess Test and undertake a dangerous journey to the east side of the island, where eight princesses help her discover what it truly means to be a princess.
  ISBN 978-1-61858-015-3
  [1. Princesses--Fiction. 2. Examinations--Fiction. 3. Islands--Fiction. 4. Orphans--Fiction. 5. Diaries--Fiction. 6. African Americans--Fiction.] I. Williams, Caroline Randall. II. Title. III. Title: Diary of B. B. Bright, possible princess. IV. Title: Diary of BeeBee Bright, possible princess.
  PZ7.R15537Di 2012
  [Fic]--dc23
                              2012014192

Manufactured by Thomson-Shore, Dexter, MI (USA); RMA584LS218, August, 2012

The Diary

of

B. B. Bright,

Possible Princess

Dear Diary,

I want off this island. If I can't step off by myself, I hope maybe I can sneak you, diary, into the bottom of one of the crates of honey we bottle and ship out every month to The Other World.

If some girl finds this diary, maybe she'll write to me and I'll have a friend. I WANT A FRIEND! A girl. My age! Or maybe some boy will find you, read you, fall in love with ME, then rush over to the island to meet me NO MATTER WHAT.

And I want to take off the necklace with the huge dark-star they make me wear every hour of every day!

None of that's going to happen. I'm going to be stuck on this island forever! Unless I can smuggle you out—and someone comes. FOR ME!

If I smuggle you out, I will have to copy you first and unspill the beans. If I tell everything, I'll be breaking one of The Three Big Rules.

Compared to breaking one of The Three Big Rules, smuggling is No Big Deal.

Randall and Randall Williams

I've got to try something. I can't take one more day alone on this island with three old ladies, two dogs, one tutor, a whole bunch of bees, and a posse of fireflies, no matter how much I love them. And I want somebody who doesn't live on this island to know I really truly am Black Bee Bright, Daughter of the Raven King and Raven Queen, even if that does break Big Rule Three.

Ouch. I just got stung. When my bees sting me they think we're kissing. Lucky I'm not allergic. Ever since a queen bee stung me my first day on the island when I was four, bees have liked me. Bees and fireflies. We get each other. The Godmother Elizabethanne calls it a "special affinity." Seven fireflies are blinking around me right now. I can't count the guard bees in the dark. But I can hear them buzz. They watch over me while I'm sleeping.

Since I'm not sleeping I wish they would chill.

Yours truly,
Me, B.bee

2

Dear Diary,

You may be wondering how it came to be that I am living on an island in the middle of very tropical nowhere. Before I EXPLAIN I've got to COMPLAIN!

All this nature was fine when I was four. Even when I was eight. In a week, I'll be THIRTEEN. I want air conditioning. I want window screens. I want a Forever Best Friend, and a Boyfriend!

I don't want to just read about those things in magazines that come six months late and in old books tucked here and there and everywhere on shelves all over our side of the island! And I don't want to spend my days helping tend beehives, playing chess, doing yoga, and studying, studying, studying! With no age-mates!

The Godmommies are beginning to get it. I tell the Godmommies I want to go to school and study with other girls. That I want to go to church and sing in a children's choir with other children and go on a Sunday School outing to an amusement park. I want to see a city, eat in a restaurant, go to a museum. When I say stuff like that, I can feel myself getting closer and closer to OFF THE ISLAND. Or at least I think I can.

The Godmommies start talking about Detroit. And San Francisco. And Harlem. They talk about big church hats on Sunday and schools where the teacher would hit your hand with a ruler if you talked out of turn and restaurants that sold pizza and restaurants with rolling carts full of little taste treasures called dim sum, and before I know it, they are talking about what it would take to hide me and keep me safe in The Other World.

Too bad I decided to share ALL my reasons with them at dinner earlier tonight. Fortunately, I didn't start with the biggies, Forever Best Friend and Boyfriend.

I started with a small one. Between sips of kale broth, I said, "I want clothes that aren't out of style in The Other World by the time the boat gets here." The Godmommies said they do not "find that argument persuasive." They threatened to cut off my subscriptions to all my glossy Other World magazines. They told me to eat my sweet potatoes.

Or, to be more precise (Mamselle says precision is important to potential princesses), Godmother Elizabeth-anne, who used to be a lawyer, told me my argument was not very persuasive. Godmother Grace, who used to be a preacher, threatened to cut off my magazines, and G. Mama Dot, who once was a bus driver and doesn't "take no stuff from nobody," told me to eat my sweet potatoes.

As far as the Godmommies are concerned, the only things I should ever read from The Other World (a boat comes once a month to bring our mail and pick up our honey) are written by Langston Hughes, Zora Neale Hurston, Will Shakespeare, Emily Dickinson, William Blake, or Gwendolyn Brooks. Or, it's in the Bible.

And the Godmommies are not impressed by what they refer to as my "sartorial challenges."

They say I look pretty in a pareo. What do you think?

Love,
BeeBee

Randall and Randall Williams

3

Dear Diary,

I just crawled out of the closet. The Godmommies are downstairs arguing. About me. Again! It's their favorite after-dinner occupation. They sit in the dark and they argue. I huddle under my covers knitting and listening, pretending to be asleep. Or I crawl into a closet if I don't want to listen.

They are arguing about whether I am more likely to find the eight princesses on this side of the island—the West Side—or on the other side, the East Side. Considering the ten-mile-wide desert that we would have to sleep right in the middle of to get to the East Side, AND considering there's nothing on the East Side of the island but a giant thorny thicket, a group of bears, and too many poisonous snakes to count (because of the East Island bear cave and snake breeding pit), I'm still hoping I can find the princesses on this side of the island. I would like to agree with G. Mama Dot, who loudly announced, "Get with it! No family forays into the thicket!" But I can't agree. I've been

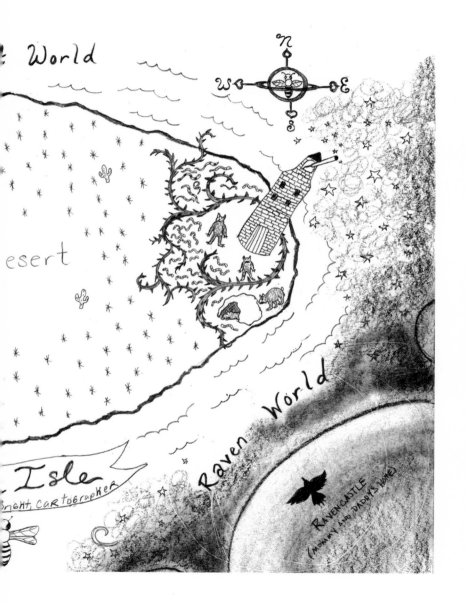

wandering around Bee Isle for eight years—since I was three or four. If there were eight princesses on this side of the island I would have found them by now! But downstairs G.Mama Dot is laying it down hot and loud how I will find the princesses on this side of the island.

Even though I can't see it, I can just imagine them downstairs wagging a short fat finger (G.Mama Dot), or a long thin finger (Godmother Elizabethanne), or a finger with lots of rings on it (Godmommy Grace), right in each others' faces. When they finger wag, they call it signifying. I call it old lady-ing.

When the Godmommies argue about how they're raising me it makes me laugh. When they talk about the things they miss because they're stuck on this island taking care of me, it makes me want to cry.

Tonight they did both, but they started with what they missed. That's why I crawled into the closet. I didn't want to hear.

They never argue or talk about things they miss in the room with me. But sometimes when they think I'm for real asleep and they think I for real can't hear, they start talking about things they miss and they get excited. And when they get excited my Godmommies get loud. I don't think they know how loud they get. Sometimes they wake me up even when I have been asleep. They are that loud.

I can hear them through three walls and two doors. They talk about stuff like Miles Davis and Ella Fitzgerald and stuff like book clubs and big church on Sunday and cable TV; and good meals they don't have to cook and libraries and the Internet. And steak and barbecue and fried chicken.

On the island we have chickens for eggs but we don't eat the chickens. And there aren't any cows or pigs. We eat fish. And lots of beans. Black-eyed peas. Red beans. Green lentils. And lots of eggs. Sometimes the eggs are turned into frittatas that are flat and dense, sometimes into soufflés that are tall and puffy, sometimes they are handkerchief-thin crepes—but it's all eggs. We eat so many eggs I call us eggatarians. When I'm old I will be talking about frittatas and soufflés and crepes like late at night they talk about ribs and chicken with waffles.

When they talk about stuff they miss for too long, Godmother Elizabethanne says, "There may be a loophole around the rules but I haven't found it yet." And just after that Godmommy Grace says, "Don't stop singing the 'Exile Blues' or we'll be stuck in them." G.Mama Dot always says, "Blues shoes, don't loose."

Fortunately they got off point and got quieter. That's when I got out of the closet. Then they got loud and interesting. They wound up arguing about raising me.

When they argue about raising me, this island is not boring. Sometimes I say things just to get them mad. I try to keep the island as interesting as I can.

Right now, Godmommy Grace is saying I don't understand anything about signifying and they should stop doing it because it scares me. G.Mama Dot says, "Baby girl owns Raven World, nothing can pierce her fierce." God-mother Elizabethanne says signifying and head bobbing is stereotypical behavior that they shouldn't be validating. Then Godmommy Grace contradicts her and says signifying is part of the armor that will help enemies fail to see—despite all other signs and appearances—that *she* (meaning *me*) is a princess.

They're talking so loud it sounds like a party. I don't know how they can think I can sleep through all their chatter and laughter and worrying.

I'm going to try.

Sleepy,
B. B.

4

Dear Diary,

I can't sleep so I'm up in bed under the covers writing in you. I'm under the covers because Mamselle, my tutor, goes out prowling at night. If she ever sees a light in my bedroom, she tells on me to the Godmommies.

My bedroom is on the third floor of the Godmommies' Cottages. The Godmommies live in three houses right next to each other: one is short and wide, one is tall and thin, and one is perfectly square. Pretty much just like the God-mommies. The tall cottage one has five stories.

I'll draw it for you.

They knocked down the walls separating their third floors to make me one huge bedroom playroom. My room's gigantic. Their bedrooms are just below mine on their separate second floors. On the first floor there's a kitchen we all use in G.Mama Dot's house. The other two have offices on their first floors.

It used to be that when they talked in the kitchen, it was hard for me to hear them. Not anymore.

G. Mama Dot just hollered something about teaching me true good manners, and about the importance of Proper Home Training.

I'm starting to wonder if maybe they're losing their hearing along with their minds. They're getting old. I don't know their exact ages but I think the Godmommies are in their late sixties or maybe seventies and even possibly eighties, and that's starting to get up there. But maybe not for Godmommies. I think they need to get up off this island as much as I do.

When I ask them how old they are, they never tell me. They say that's one of the special things about being a woman of color—you look young longer. They say, "Black don't crack."

They say I have skin the color of honey and eyes the

color of chocolate, and lips the color of plums. They say I am the prettiest princess of all.

I don't feel very pretty. I have a zit, I have funny hair, AND I have odd clothes, if you can even call a pareo "clothes" in the plural. My skin may be the color of chocolate; my lips, plums; and my eyes, honey; but it comes together funny. The evidence? I don't have a best friend or a boyfriend.

I say all of this in my head; I don't say it out loud. Out loud, I laugh and say I look pretty good in a pareo. If they don't know their godchild isn't pretty, I don't want to be the one to tell them.

I love the Godmommies. Mainly I just want to be exactly like them. Who wouldn't? G.Mama Dot, the one who says everything in rhymes, was a gonna-be hip-hop artist and an everyday bus driver when she lived in The Other World. Now she paints. She lives in the short, wide house. Godmother Elizabethanne plays chess with me and helps me figure out every kind of puzzle and plan. She was a lawyer. She lives in the tall, skinny house. Godmommy Grace was a preacher. She's really good at listening, and she does yoga. She teaches me yoga. She lives in the square house. And Godmother Elizabethanne plays chess . . . I said that already, but that's kinda sorta just like living on the island: you get back to the things you just did quick. Too quick.

Love, Me

P.S. The Godmommies are beautiful. I think it's easier to be beautiful when you're old.

Dear Diary,

This morning the Godmommies got back to the subject of my clothes, too quick. When the Godmommies start telling, again, some story about some old great-aunt down in some small town in Alabama, maybe Tuskegee, who had to put her outfits together from a "poor barrel" (a giant barrel of used clothes), shipped South from a church in the North, I want them to stop. Somehow the fact that that girl managed to turn herself into the best-dressed girl in a town—even though some of the rich girls shopped in fancy Birmingham department stores—makes me feel silly and selfish, and just plain less-than.

But silly and selfish and less-than though it be, I want to say I'm tired of hearing stories about distant relatives. If they *are* relatives! Is a God-cousin a relative? I want to say I don't believe them. I want to say they make up these stories to PERSECUTE ME. To drive me just BANANAS. Because I don't have friends or clothes—even from a poor barrel. But I don't say any of that, I just let myself know I *want* to say it.

I also don't say I never see pictures of other girls running around wrapped in a piece of silk or cotton in the pages of my magazines—except for maybe girls just getting out of a bath or a shower wrapped up in a towel.

Godmother Elizabethanne tried to reason with me. She always tries to reason with me. She said I might not have the clothes I want, but I do have the most beautiful jewelry of any girl she has ever known. Godmother Elizabethanne had a point.

My necklace is pretty amazing. It's a gold chain with one giant darkstar in the middle and four other jewels on either side. The aunts say the little stones are a ruby, a pearl, an amber bead, a garnet, a jasper bead, a topaz, a sapphire, and a padpararadscha. One stone is see-through red, one is solid white, one is clear golden, one is clear dark red, one is a mottled purple, one is a grayish shade of clear golden, one is clear blue, and one is a clear pinky shade of orange. The necklace is pretty pretty. Except I've worn it every day of my life. Because of that it's boring. And it doesn't look anything like anything any girls in my magazines wear. So I get back to my point. Way out loud. And from a different angle.

I say, "I want normal jewelry!"

They say, "Hush!"

This makes me mad. The Godmommies are always saying the truth will set me free. I tell the truth as often as I can and I'm still in prison on the prettiest island in the world—at least it's prettier than any of the other islands I've seen in the *World Book Encyclopedia* or in my magazines.

Yours,
Bee Bee

P.S. From what I've seen in the encyclopedia, Bee Isle looks like a cross between Martinique, Madagascar, and Maui, and a little like Martha's Vineyard. They should call it MMMM Isle!

6

Dear Diary,

Maybe the Godmommies meant to say big truths will set you free and little truths will get you shushed. This morning during before-breakfast yoga, while holding my buzzing-bee pose beside Godmommy Grace, I closed my eyes and tried to think of the truest truth I knew.

Something that would make the Godmommies risk breaking one of the Three Big Rules.

The first big rule is: No man can step foot on the island. The second big rule is: I can't step foot off the island until I've met eight princesses. So far I haven't met one. WE ARE GOING TO BE STUCK ON THIS ISLAND FOREVER. The third big rule is: I can't tell anyone I'm the Raven King's daughter. I hate The Three Big Rules.

If a man steps foot on the island, he will disappear. No one knows exactly how long it will take each time, but the Godmommies guess it would be somewhere between immediately and less than a day. The time I saw it: ten seconds.

And if I step foot off the island before meeting the eight princesses, I will disappear. Probably immediately.

I've been waiting to meet the princesses for so long and not one has shown her face. I don't even really want to meet them anymore. I just want to get off the island.

The punishment for breaking Rule Three is trickier; no one knows what it is. It could be something small like all the blueberries on the island disappear. Or it could be really big, like I get killed by someone who thinks I might be the rightful heir to the Raven Throne.

Rule Three is a biggie. Even G.Mama Dot who doesn't get scared is afraid of Rule Three. She got so afraid she threatened me. She said, "Child, I don't know what ELSE will happen if you EVER tell ANYONE you are the Raven King's daughter—but one thing for sure will happen, I will snatch your bald head!"

I don't think G.Mama Dot would harm a hair on my head. But she threatens to. When she threatens to "snatch my bald head" I know I am absolutely not supposed to do whatever she's talking about under any circumstances what-soever. I GET IT. RULE THREE is BIG!

But does it have to be? What if everyone in Raven World (one of the fairytale kingdoms) and in The Other World (the regular place where the Godmommies came from) knew I had zero intention of ever sitting on the Raven Throne? I want to write a letter to all the magical worlds in this Universe and to the regular world: *To whom it may concern, on this island, in Raven World, or in The Other World: I do not*

*want to sit in, or on, or even near my Daddy and my Mama's throne.
Period. Exclamation mark.*

I've seen what happens when someone sits on the Raven Throne who isn't supposed to. I saw two such somebodies sit on the Raven Thrones. I saw them get frozen into giant blocks of ice.

I haven't always lived on Bee Isle. My mother brought me here and hid me here when I was little. There was a war in Raven World. That's where I was born, where I lived in a stone castle 36 meters tall and 21 meters wide. Where my father was a king. Where my mother was a queen. Where I was a—I can't tell you. We think my parents got killed in that war.

Godmommy Grace says if my parents got killed they are in heaven and they are with me all the time, even if I can't see them. I don't think my parents got killed. It doesn't feel like they're with me all the time.

Godmother Elizabethanne thinks my parents may have moved to The Other World and have not found a safe way to come back and get me. Safe for me, she means. G.Mama Dot says, "No way to know, baby, no way to know." I love the way G.Mama talks. It sounds like a low rumbling song. That's something I know. And there's something else I do know.

I had a friend in Ravencastle. A boy. His name was Enchantment. When I first came to Bee Isle, I would tell the Godmommies stories about me and that boy. We would play hide-and-seek, and tic-tac-toe, and have thumb battles for hours. The first year I was here, when I was so sad about having nobody to play with, I wrote a book, *Zip and Zap*. I said the words out loud and Godmother Elizabethanne wrote them down and G.Mama Dot held the crayons while I drew the pictures. It was full of pictures of things that boy and I did at Ravencastle, and now I don't even remember his whole name. But I remember hiding behind some curtains in the throne room when that boy and I were playing freeze tag and seeing my cousin and his wife get frozen into giant ice blocks FOREVER when they did what they weren't supposed to do and tried to sit on the Raven Thrones.

And I know what happened to my parents—they sat on the Raven Thrones and they disappeared. Not immediately. Not into a block of ice. But from my life!

If ever I get off this island, I am not putting one foot on even the bottom rung of either of the velvet carpeted ebony stairs leading to the two Raven Thrones.

I'm going to stay on permanent vaycay!

Godmother Elizabethanne says, "Perpetual vacation is for the dissolute and willing to be bored." She says it so often I have memorized the sentence forwards and backwards, "Bored be to willing and dissolute the for is vacation perpetual." Godmother Elizabethanne says permanent vaycay is for the kind of princesses who *inherit* but don't *inhabit* their office. *Whatever. That. Means. Ugh.* But when G.Mama Dot says that whether or not I'm going to try for the throne, there are people who would want to kill anybody who has any chance of being heir to my father's kingdom, I listen. I can't break Big Rule Three. Rule Three is important. They say the nearer I get to the age I can sit on the throne, the more important it gets to not break Rule Three.

Mamselle says the closer I get to taking the OPT the more important Rule Three gets.

The OPT is one of the reasons the Godmommies are fighting with Mamselle these days. Mainly I'm home-schooled by the Godmommies. But the Godmommies invited Mamselle to the island to tutor me in things royal in preparation for the OPT.

The OPT (Official Princess Test) allows any girl to be acknowledged as princess without having to be born royal, to be adopted by a royal, or to marry a royal. If I'm not allowed to tell anyone I'm the Raven King's daughter, and I want to be a princess, I have to take the OPT. If I pass the OPT, I will be called Princess Bee Bee. Or, B. B. Bright, Princess of Light. Something that doesn't reveal what the Godmommies sniff and call "my origins." Such as Black Bee Bright, Princess of Ravencastle. If I want to be acknowledged as a princess but I don't want to break Rule Three, I've got to pass the OPT.

But, and this is a huge *but,* if I take the OPT and don't pass it, I'm no longer any princess at all!

A girl who fails the OPT cannot be a princess. Even if she marries a prince. Even if she marries a king. Even if she was born a princess. Even if she is adopted by a princely family. A girl who fails the OPT cannot be a princess. The OPT is scary.

25

That's why they're paying almost all the money they are making from their honey company to Mamselle to tutor me. I have to pass. Only a girl who has passed the OPT can travel between the three worlds and into and out of fairytale time.

Unfortunately for me, even if I do pass the OPT, I won't be able to travel anywhere because I haven't met the Eight Princesses. The Godmommies say, "First things first. Pass the OPT."

The Godmommies are not certain Mamselle's preparing me correctly. They want their "money's worth." They do not want me to lose options.

And G.Mama Dot and Godmother Elizabethanne are mad with Mamselle for siding with Godmommy Grace in the argument about whether I will have to go to the other side of the island to find the Princesses. I'm a little mad at Godmommy Grace and Mamselle for thinking I need to go over to the East Side of the island. Desert. Bears. Snakes. Ugh!!! But G.Mama Dot's got my back. She shoots down all notions of me going to East Island anytime soon.

G.Mama Dot snapped her fingers loud, and in a deep voice she said, "Mamselle's gyrating is eye-rotating irritating!" Godmommy Grace laughed her high-pitched laugh that sounded a little like a bird cry and a lot like she was about to say something important, then she kept her ideas to herself. Godmother Elizabethanne said, "Mamselle is B. B.'s staunch advocate!"

Mamselle arrived on my eighth birthday. She lives in a

house that looks like a miniature French chateau on the beach. Before Mamselle arrived that little building was the boathouse.

Mamselle is very pretty, very quiet, and very mysterious. She's not Other World like the Godmommies; she's Fairytale—and just a little strange. She tells me she is almost four hundred years old, but the Godmommies say she looks like she's thirty. That's strange. And she keeps a miniature horse as a pet. His name is Bayard. When Bayard's in the house he wears a kind of diaper. Mamselle wears the kind of clothes I see in my Other World magazines except all of her clothes are black. Most of them are names I can't quite say, but I can tell you this, Diary: Mamselle is fancy. Very, very fancy . . .

The Godmommies, particularly G.Mama Dot and Godmother Elizabethanne, who are funky-fun, down-to-earth, and loudly glamorous, worry that, even though they invited her, Mamselle is a spy coming to sabotage my future performance on the Princess Test. I worry that the Godmommies are getting paranoid.

It's not always fun being Black Bee Bright, Princess of Light, daughter of the Raven King and Queen and probable heir to the Raven Throne.

There, I did it. Broke Big Rule Three. Inadvertently. (My new word for the day.)

Breaking the rule wasn't as much fun as I thought it would be. Maybe writing in you, Diary, doesn't count. I would prefer to break Big Rule Two.

And maybe if I don't step foot off the island but am carried off to a boat, I might not disappear. Or maybe I could ride Mamselle's tiny horse up the gangplank of a boat. I want to see The Other World. And maybe find my parents if they are still alive. But more than that I want to see Ravencastle and Raven World. The place they loved above all other places, the place that is my home. The place they probably died trying to save.

I will find a way home or disappear trying. I am my mother's daughter. I will risk return. I will find a way or make a way home.

Love,
Black Bee Bright, Possible Princess of Light

P.S. Don't tell anyone I'm the Raven King's daughter. Just send a boy, preferably not a prince, who wants to meet a wild girl in a pareo.

7

Dear Diary,

I hope maybe the Duke (Mamselle says a Duke is ruling Ravencastle and has sent spies to find me) sends a young spy who falls in love with me, then double crosses the Duke. Or maybe the Duke will send an Ambassador and not a spy and the Ambassador will tell me that the Duke wants to find me and return me to my rightful place, not find me and kill me. The Godmommies don't agree. G. Mama Dot says: "You green!" Godmother Elizabeth-anne says: "You are naïve." Godmommy Grace says: "You are in the throes of inheritance idealism." *Yeah. Okay.* I'm probably wrong about the Ambassador.

I say at least I'm not paranoid. I say maybe there's been a revolution and democracy has been established in Ravencastle and I can return as a regular citizen and it IS safe for us to return to Raven Kingdom. The Godmommies say, "And maybe not."

I like the idea of democracy. I think it's pretty inevitable and might have even come to Raven World.

Randall and Randall Williams

Godmother Elizabethanne praises my analysis but says we need more information before we can sally forth.

The Godmommies talk strange. One talks in hip-hop; one talks very, very logically; and one talks kind of preachy and old fashioned. I talk like my magazines mixed up with my daily vocabulary words. And some like the Godmommies.

I want to meet some people my own age. I want a best friend who does not have wings or walk around on four legs. And when I meet them I want to sound normal. Fat chance.

My best friends on this island are Rotty, a rottweiler who came with the Godmommies, and Zuzu, a shih tzu, who came to the island with my mother when she lived on the East Side of the island before she met my father, and my fireflies and my bees. I want a friend who's a little more like me.

They get that. When I worry the Godmommies by "talking incessantly" (that's what Godmother Elizabethanne calls it when I go on and on) to a pretend friend who I pretend looks exactly like me and is just my age and starts acting all jealous about Huck Finn and Tom Sawyer or Harriet and Sport or Harriet and Beth Ellen Hansen, I can, to use a phrase all the Godmommies are always using, "taste the end of exile." (I know I'm too old to talk to imaginary folk, but this girl needs to talk to someone her age—sometimes—and there's nobody my age who's real on this island.)

I can almost see us moving up the gangway (me carried,

of course, or on the tiny horse) onto a boat ready to set sail across the Orange Sea for The Other World or Raven World. Every time I suggest this as a possibility, they say it's too risky to try.

I once got them so close to being ready to risk it. We were sitting with the candles burning particularly bright. Then the candles burned out and they got cautious again. So we were sitting in the dark like we usually did—they didn't like to waste candles (they say the island bees work too hard to waste wax or honey). They said I should leave the island on my own two feet. After I meet the Eight Princesses. When I'm ready and the world is ready.

I started begging to leave the island. Now! When I begged, the Godmommies got tears in their eyes. I won't beg again.

I think I misunderstood that Temptations song the Godmommies sing while washing up our breakfast dishes. I should have paid more attention to the part that goes, "I've heard a crying man is half a man, with no sense of pride" instead of to the title, "Ain't Too Proud to Beg." Next time.

Night, night,
Black Bee Bright

Dear Diary,

First I beat G. Mama Dot, then I beat Godmommy Grace at chess today! Little Whoopdedoo! Then I beat Godmother Elizabethanne. *Big* Whoopdeedoo. Godmother Elizabethanne always beats me. Until today! When I beat all three of them, the Godmommies started singing and dancing around the kitchen a song about me being the sunshine of their life. The Godmommies are a little crazy.

I think they've been on the island too long with no break.

It was supposed to be their retirement half-year vacation place. The year I was born my mother started to hear stories about triplets who lived in The Other World. A bus driver, a lawyer, and a preacher who lived in Detroit, Michigan. They had done so much good work in their community that they had gotten on the wrong side of more than one gang and even the police. Mama told them, and they told me, that she believed even great warriors needed places of safe retreat. She invited the triplets to live part of each year in the three little cottages she had built for them by the Purple Lake in her secret place, Bee Isle. She used her magic to get them here.

Then war came to Raven World and Mama brought me back to the one place she believed I would be safe. I don't know how it was she didn't figure in the boring part. She had lived on the island herself. I guess she forgot.

If there had been Three Big Rules back then I wouldn't have been born. But that's not exactly right. Daddy came to the island as a bird, or so the Godmommies told me. The Godmommies also say Mama knew the Eight Princesses. And she never told anyone she was the Raven Queen's daughter . . . because she wasn't. Mama obeyed the rules. And she didn't know who her daddy was and her mama was mean. Mama didn't have it easy.

That was then. This is too hard. Now. On me and the Godmommies. The blues of exile. They've got that. I've got it too. And I've got the I-want-a-boyfriend-blues. They say I'm too young to have that. The Godmommies don't know everything.

Yesterday, after holding the flickering firefly pose for half an hour, I spoke my deepest truth *knowing* it would set us all free. That we'd be on the next boat for The Other World. I said, "I WANT A BOYFRIEND."

Wrong Move.

Even though I didn't add, a boyfriend like in the magazines, from The Other World, I think they figured it out.

33

Randall and Randall Williams

The Godmommies say me wanting a boyfriend at twelve years young makes them glad we live on an island. They say it's fine and even good for me to want one—and it's their job to make sure I don't have one until I'm old enough to "make the right decisions."

When they say "make the right decisions," I can hear, and I mean actually, literally, hear, trumpets blaring. Just after they get the words out: *dunt-ta-ta-dun*, putting an exclamation point on the sentence, *dunt-ta-ta-dun!*

That's just one of the strange things that happens each day just to remind me this is a magic place.

The Godmommies say tomorrow we're going to bake honeycake as well as make honey. That we will have our own pre-birthday Honey Festival. Right!

We are not on vacation; we are in exile, on a fourteen-mile-wide island where it is always warm and most of the trees are palm trees. Sometimes the water around our island turns bright orange or red. I think that's because the island is magical. Godmother Elizabethanne says it's because there are that many fluorescent fish swimming in it. My mother named me after this place.

In my universe there are three worlds: The Other World, Raven World, and Bright World. The worlds touch in strange ways and places. People from The Other World can travel to Bright World. And people from Bright World can travel to Raven World. But people from The Other World can't travel to Raven World. And people from Raven World can't travel to The Other World.

Unless you pass the OPT, the Godmommies say, who learned this from Mamselle.

The Godmommies aren't really my godmothers; they are my guardians. And I don't mean like lawyers—I mean like ninja warriors, except imagine black ladies. They are here to protect me. So is Rotty. He's a downtown Detroit rottweiler. Badder than that Leroy Brown G.Mama Dot is always humming about.

I say it would be safe to be with them in The Other World. They say I don't know what I'm talking about.

I'm not mentioning boyfriends again. I am going to fill up the pages of this book and smuggle it out and hope maybe someone reading this wants to visit this magic place.

I hope some cute boy comes to find me on this island—even if he knows that he'll disappear shortly after stepping foot on Bee Isle and I'm going to disappear when we step off.

Yours truly,
Black Bee Bright

9

Dear Diary,

The Godmommies say an invisible prince would be way worse than no prince at all. They won't even talk about me being an invisible princess.

I stop talking about boyfriends and start talking about being bored with just being a honey-making assistant.

The Godmommies make honey and ship it to The Other World with a label on it that reads *Island Honey*. And there's a picture of a palm tree. People think it comes from Hawaii. It comes from our island, Bee Isle. The Godmommies have a lot of fun with their business. And they make a little money that they send to friends in need in The Other World.

I want to start a business of my own—and I don't mean a little old lavender lemonade stand like I had when I was six and seven and eight. My last stand was when I was eight. Mamselle had just arrived. I sold her a glass. Then I sold one to G.Mama Dot and Mamselle's eyebrows raised so high I thought they had levitated into her hairline. But she didn't say a word. She didn't have to say a word, I knew. I knew the Godmommies do too much for me for me to charge them for anything. So I gave G.Mama Dot her glass for free, and Mamselle's eyebrows dropped down to where they belonged. She said to G.Mama, "B. B. is quite coachable." Even without coaching, I know I need some customers I don't know AND a good idea for a business. I tell the Godmommies, "I need a good idea for a business." All they say is, "All in good time, precious, all in good time."

I snap back, trying not to sound or look too sassy, "The best time is now."

"The best time is now," is a phrase the Godmommies taught me. I learned early on that fighting fire with fire in Bright World usually means fighting the Godmommies' words with the Godmommies' words.

I followed that little verbal jab with a sidekick, mentioning that having my own company might just make me seem less like a princess. If it did, it would, in fact, support Big Rule Three.

I got the Godmommies so dizzy with my contradictory arguments and their contradictory statements and so happy with knowing I was thinking about something other than boys and clothes, they gave in.

Tomorrow I've got to think of a business to start. Except tomorrow is MY BIRTHDAY. I will start my business the day after tomorrow.

Goodnight,
Black Bee Bright

Dear Diary,

HAPPY BIRTHDAY TO ME. I am THIRTEEN! After a breakfast of blueberry and apricot and mint salad with toast hearts spread with honey, the Godmommies gave me a poem to go with my necklace.

> *Ruby is fair of face,*
> *Tope is full of grace.*
> *Ammie is full of woe,*
> *Jaz has far to go.*
> *Gigi and ChaCha are loving and giving.*
> *Sass and Pearl work hard for a living.*
> *But the child who is born on the seventh day*
> *Is bright with the light of all these ways.*

The poem was signed "Love, Mama."
     The poem makes me want to cry. Well, not the poem, the way the author signed it part, the "Love, Mama" part.

Turning thirteen is not as fun as I thought it was going to be. I miss my mother. I miss other people I can barely remember. I'm sad. I'm bored. I want to do something, but I don't know what I want to do.

So I ran out of the kitchen without saying thank you or excuse me. The Godmommies didn't say a word. I guess it was because it was my birthday.

I took a long walk with Zuzu down to the pebble beach below Mamselle's house. Because it is my birthday there are no lessons today. As I approached Mamselle's house I started singing—loudly. I was so mad I wanted her to peek out to greet me just so I could ignore her. I wanted every single person on West Island to know just how frustrating it is to be stuck on an island with no one else your age the day you turn thirteen. Loud as I raised my voice, I didn't raise Mamselle. Her door stayed shut like her window shades.

Fortunately the moment Zuzu's paws hit the pebble beach she started looking for a stick of driftwood. It only took her a minute to find one and drop it at my feet, barking.

When Zuzu and I go walking by the beach, I always throw a stick out into the water. Then Zuzu trots into the waves and paddles out to the stick. When she returns to me with the stick in her mouth, first she shakes real hard, getting me wet, then she drops the stick at my feet.

I think Zuzu comes so close and shakes so hard because she wants me to know even a little bit what the ocean feels like and how the ocean tastes. I love Zuzu.

Randall and Randall Williams

The Godmommies say sometimes the only way to get over feeling real sorry for yourself is to settle in somewhere private and give yourself a great big pity party. So I did. I went all the way. I said to myself, I think I'd rather be a dog than a girl. Zuzu can step off the island. I said to myself, I envy Zuzu. I said so many things like that I bored myself. It was time for me to close the conversation, with the three magic words I always use to snap myself out of pity parties: "Get over it!"

When I came back from my walk with Zuzu the Godmommies pretended like I had never left.

Off to help a little with the hives even if it is my birthday,

Beebee-who-doesn't-have-one-thing-in-her-life-the-way-she-wants-it.

P.S. I'm starting to notice it's on days that I particularly want everything to go exactly right, everything starts going exactly wrong. I am going to stop wanting things to be perfect. But first I'm going to eat lunch.

Dear Diary,

After lunch—elvish honeycakes from our Tolkien cook-book—the Godmommies had the most wonderful surprise for me, something they called "spa day."

First they gave me a spa-kini to wear. And they cocooned my necklace in gauze. Then they washed my hair with an egg and sweet-smelling soaps. When my hair was what they called "clean," they put mayonnaise all over it and wrapped it in a towel.

After that, they put me in a bathtub full of salts and lav-ender leaves and let me soak. While I was soaking they put cucumber slices over my eyes. The Godmommies pulled my feet out of the water. One Godmommy took one foot and one took the other. They scrubbed my feet with salt and oatmeal while the third Godmommy stuck one, then the other of my elbows in half-lemons.

Because there were cucumbers on my eyes I couldn't tell who was who and who did what. All the while they were work-ing on me they sang old rhythm-and-blues songs and Beatles

41

songs. They sang "Shop Around," "The Way You Do the Things You Do," "How Sweet It Is," and "I Feel Good."

After I got out of the tub, and after they rinsed the mayonnaise, and salt, and lemon juice, and cucumber off of me, my spa-kini, and my hair, they wrapped me in a robe and painted my fingernails and my toenails.

Once I was what they called "shiny and new," they uncocooned my necklace and polished the stones with clean gauze. Just as the darkstar got its last buff, Godmother Elizabethanne said, "You were born on the seventh day."

Then Godmommy Grace said, "Truth."

And G.Mama Dot said, "Word."

Then they kissed me and the island said a literal *ta-da!* I took that as my cue to run up to my room to get out of my wet spa-kini and get properly dressed for my birthday dinner.

I want to wear something wild and weird, something like the outfits I see in my magazines, but I don't think it's wise to be too disobedient on a day when you are in full expectation of receiving more presents. That would be— disrespectful. Churlish. Unnecessary. And plain not nice to the Godmommies, whom I do adore.

In honor of the Godmommies I will be wearing my prettiest pareo. Even if I feel, after being covered in egg and mayonnaise and lemon, a little like a Caesar salad.

Yours,
Not-so-bossy BeeBee

12

Dear Diary,

Dinner was delish. Because it was my special day we had a
guest, Mamselle, and the Godmommies served the meal up-
side down. We had dessert first, honey fresh from the combs
with Mamselle's madeleines. The madeleines looked like
puffy seashell cupcakes. They tasted a little like pound cake if
pound cake tasted like oranges and flowers as well as like
vanilla and butter and sugar. I loved them. The madeleines
were followed by the main course, sweet potato soufflé. For
dessert we ate our appetizer, island herb salad.

After dins we all (Mamselle, the Godmommies, and me)
cleared the dirty dishes, and I opened presents in the candlelight at the big table.

Each of the Godmommies gave me what they called a
little present and together they gave me a big present.

My little presents were great. I got a chessboard, a yoga
mat, and a Bible. My big present was amazing—a quilt the
Godmommies had worked on together. Each row of the
quilt had six squares in it. And the quilt was six squares

long so the quilt itself was one big square. Nine of the squares had pictures and the rest were pretty colors. The pictures were a book, a heart, a circle with a baby in it, an infinity symbol, a throne, a leaf, a rainbow-colored number five, a paintbrush, and a nine-pointed black star.

"A very special story quilt."

"It's beautiful."

"Want to know why it's special?"

"Yes."

"Most story quilts tell the story of the past."

"Your quilt tells the future."

"Whose future?"

"Yours, silly."

"Mine?"

"Yours. Of course."

"Read it to me."

"Only you can read it."

"I can't read it."

"One day you will be able to."

"When will that day be?"

"Only time will tell."

"Until you are able to read the quilt, keep it near. Once a story quilt is sewn and given, read or unread, it provides the girl it belongs to special shelter and protection."

"Wow."

It was a pretty silly thing to say but it was the only thing I could think of that made sense. Wow. Good Wow.

The quilt is beautiful. I am laying under it as I write. Safe and excited at the very same time.

Beaming Birthday Bright,
B. B.

13

Dear Diary,

Because I turned thirteen yesterday, today Godmommy Grace taught me a whole new series of yoga poses. The real ones. Downward dog. Cat and Cow and Warrior One and Warrior Two. Downward dog is cool. Your hands and feet are on the ground and your butt is in the air. And there are boring ones like tree. Tree is when you just stand in the middle of your yoga mat and feel your feet and make sure your tongue is not stuck to the top of your mouth. Godmother Elizabethanne says to do that you just yawn with your lips together. I just did it. Kept my mouth closed but yawned. When I'm writing I get so excited my tongue gets jammed to the roof of my mouth. Close lips and yawn and it's down again. Godmother Elizabethanne says unsticking my tongue from the roof of my mouth will help me relax and do my best on the OPT.

I told her I just needed to relax and get through the last

of Mamselle's intensive review sitting on either side of her double-sided partners desk.

The thing I like best about Mamselle's house is that she has a painting of my Mama. Mama's portrait hangs on the wall between paintings of Rapunzel, Sleeping Beauty, Cinderella, and The Princess of Cleves. Each painting is in a gold frame. It's easy to tell who's who—the names are printed on the gold with black ink in flowy script. Princess calligraphy. I was especially happy to see Mama's portrait today.

In front of the portraits is a big round table covered in a shiny cloth that hangs to the ground. The table is covered with photographs in silver frames. Some of the photos are of a small group of girls wearing the very same princess uniform. And there were large group photos of whole princess school classes.

I can never keep the names of those girls in the group photos straight. Mamselle has told me their names a hundred times, but they get jumbled. In their uniforms they all look like the same girl—a girl who I don't ever think will be me. But the picture of Mama keeps me keepin' on, as G.Mama Dot would say.

Once we settled down into our seats on opposites of the big wooden desk, we worked on all five areas of the OPT but smushed together like they would be on the real test. Usually we just work on the five areas—Languages and History; Problem Solving; Character; Poise; and Persuasion— separately. Languages and History is the hardest. There's so much to memorize. Verbs. Dates. How to greet people and how to take leave of people in dozens upon dozens of languages. So much.

For today's practice test Mamselle asked me to choose a queen to defend as the greatest queen of all time. I chose Elizabeth the First. She was very smart. Spoke many languages. Successfully protected England from foreign invasion. I was thinking the OPT would be a cinch. When the second question came: "Now make the case that Queen Elizabeth I is a very bad role model for young princesses."

"I can't make that case."

"Think! Answer!"

"I can't!"

"Can't, or won't?"

Mamselle wanted an answer and I didn't have one. I didn't even want to have an answer. Even to pass the test. Finally, I said, "I will not make the case against a queen I admire."

Mamselle stared silently. Her gray eyes did not smile. Neither did her mouth. Finally she cleared her throat and stood up—like she couldn't stand working with me for a minute longer.

She moved towards the door and to a beautiful umbrella stand she used to hold the many parasols she employed to shade her creamy brown skin from the island sun. From among the parasols she pulled out a tube all wrapped in a shiny gold and silver paper. Tube in hand, she sat back down at the double-sided desk. Then she placed the tube between us. With a smile she pushed the tube toward me. I do not believe I have ever seen Mamselle smile before. Normally her lips are a straight slash of red, but this day they curved. When I tore open the paper there was a map of our island.

"Your mother drew this map for me when she was a girl and gave it to me as a gift. Now I'm giving it to you."

I spread the map out on the desk, holding it down with both palms. Then Mamselle held one side down with her palm and I held the other with a palm.

Everything on the West Side of the island looked completely familiar: our house, Mamselle's house, the Purple Lake, the beach, the apiaries where the bees live, everything. And there was the desert separating east from west. Nothing on the East Side of the island looked familiar or foretold. There was no thicket. No giant bear caves. No snake breeding pit. Except for the lake and the boat dock (the Godmommies had mentioned a lake and a boat dock), there was nothing I had heard about. There were wildflower meadows, there were three nice-sized ponds. A second beach. And there was a Tower Castle. The Tower Castle shocked me!

"That's where your mother lived when she ruled this island," said Mamselle.

"It can't be."

"Your mother drew this map."

The Godmommies had lied to me. I don't remember a single other thing about the rest of that day's lessons except that the Godmommies had lied to me. And when I got back to the cottages I lied to the Godmommies. For the very first time. I told them the tube I had tucked up under my arm was full of my drawings. Then I told them I had worked so hard on my Greek greetings I wanted to go to bed. Early. Another lie. I really just wanted to get to my room and look at the map. I wanted to plan my march across the island.

Dishonest but not quite dastardly,
BeeBee, citizen revolutionary

14

Dear Diary,

I got up early, early, early to admit to, then apologize for, lying, but the Godmommies got up earlier. I could see them out the kitchen window wearing the funny hats with cheesecloth draping that they wear when they tend hives. There was already a pot of oatmeal simmering on the stove and a few cups of blackberries drying in a colander by the sink. All that was left for me to do was set the table. I set it with the blue and white dishes I liked best and picked a special teacup to put at each place. Though we were only four, the table was big enough for eight. I put the map on the other side of the table and sat down to look at it again.

When the Godmommies came in they all saw the map before they saw anything—even me. G.Mama Dot let out a yelp. I startled and the map rolled back up, then started rolling across the table. Godmommy Grace lunged forward and seized the map before it could roll off the table onto the floor. She lifted her chin into the

51

air and spoke looking down her nose at her sisters. Her look demanded silence.

"I think we have some explaining to do to BeeBee," said Godmommy Grace.

"All in due time, all in due time," said G.Mama Dot, who was not a woman anyone could silence.

"You are always saying, 'The best time is now,'" said Godmommy Grace.

"My map!" I said, reaching for the object in Godmommy Grace's hand. Godmommy Grace pressed the map securely into my palm. Her sisters gave Godmommy Grace a look I had never seen before, a look that said they wished Godmommy Grace would vanish off the face of our island.

"Sister, you should never have given B. B. the map without consulting us!" said Godmother Elizabethanne.

"I didn't!" said Grace.

"Who did?" asked Dot.

"Mamselle," I answered.

G.Mama Dot was furious. She was so mad she didn't even rhyme.

"That takes the cake! Whether B. B. is ready for the Court of Queens or isn't! Mamselle needs to do whatever she needs to do to get the Queens here, the test over, then Mamselle needs to step it up and go. I'm past tired of having that heifer on this island!"

G.Mama Dot was mad. But I wasn't going to let G.Mama Dot being mad distract me from my question. I was mad too.

"Why did you lie to me?"

G. Mama Dot stuck her hand out. Her tiniest finger was missing. I had noticed this before, but never before had I been told what happened.

"Pain was not pretend. I stuck a pinky in," said G. Mama Dot.

"It burst into flames," said Godmother Elizabethanne.

"And dissolved into ashes," said Godmommy Grace.

"If you go to the East Side of the island you must go alone," said Godmother Elizabethanne.

"We ain't exactly lied, we don't know what's over there," said G. Mama Dot.

"We only know what Mamselle says and what the map she has says," said Godmother Elizabethanne.

"She showed you the map?" I asked.

"When she first came," said Godmommy Grace.

"After you invited her?" I asked. I could feel another lie in the air. I wanted to know exactly where it was.

"We didn't invite her. She showed up. She said your mother told her to come. But your mother didn't say anything about her to us."

"The Raven Queen was in a terrible hurry," said Godmommy Grace.

"We made Mamselle promise not to show you the map until . . ." said Godmother Elizabethanne.

"Your thirteenth birthday," finished Godmommy Grace.

"I forgot that part," said G. Mama Dot.

53

"You wanted to forget it," I said, back talking for the very first time.

"I want the Queens here, the OPT over, and Mamselle gone!" said G. Mama Dot.

My punishment for fibbing about the map was I had to write out I will not tell lies one hundred times. My punishment for being insolent and asking the Godmommies why they didn't have to write I will not tell lies was I had to copy out the definition of insolent ten times. My natural consequence of fibbing was I had to be the one to tell Mamselle that it was time for the OPT. And I was to invite her to come to the house for a kale, black-eyed pea, and sweet-potato broth supper so that the Godmommies could give her a piece of their minds. And we could put this all in our past and move on. The Godmommies are big on moving on—except when it comes to getting off the island.

When I gave her the news, Mamselle seemed almost pleased. I guess she's ready to move on, too—especially if moving on includes my migration east.

Off to conjugate a few verbs before I get ready for dinner,

B. B.

15

Dear Diary,

Mamselle was excited. She showed up for dinner a few minutes early. The first half of the meal went well. Then we started talking about East Island.

"*When* she goes. Not *if*," said Mamselle.

"If!" said G.Mama Dot.

"She's not going," said Godmommy Grace.

"I want to see my mother's castle," I said.

No one said a word for almost a full minute after I said that. Everyone looked at me. The faces were variations of very afraid: Worried. Scared. Terrified. Alarmed. Finally, Godmother Elizabethanne spoke in a voice like a sword. "Mamselle, I wish you had done us all a favor and picked another present."

"Selection on the island is very limited," said Mamselle. Her voice was like a sword as well. Silence enveloped my little party as the verbal swords crossed.

Our candles had burned out. I slipped out of my

chair at the cantankerous table and up to my room. In my desk, I found two candles I had made earlier that day from the wax from our island bee hives. I returned to the dining table. I lit my candles. Suddenly the mood changed. The Godmommies began to laugh. Mamselle began to smile.

"Mamselle, you chose the perfect present."

"No, Godmommies! Your quilt is the perfect present."

I was pleased to see my little experiment worked. Pleased, but still curious.

"What's really on that side of the island?"

"Eight princesses."

"Who never grow old."

"Invisible at will."

"Flower-full and power-full."

"And an evil giant bear," said Godmother Elizabeth-anne, who never liked it much when the rest of us did what she called "lapse poetic." Godmother Elizabethanne lifted her shirt to show a scar.

"How did you get that if you can't go to the East Side without turning into ashes?" I asked.

Godmother Elizabethanne smiled before she answered. She loves it when I reason stuff out.

"The bear came to our side. Before I could chase him back, the immense yellowy-white beast scratched me. Animals can move between the sides," said Godmother Elizabethanne.

"And royals."

"Whether or not you take the OPT you are Black Bee Bright, Princess of Unstated Territory. You could go," said Godmommy Grace.

"At least until I fail the OPT," I said.

"I think we should give Miss Bee our permission to set off for East Island *after* she takes the Princess Test," said Godmother Elizabethanne, looking to Mamselle and Godmommy Grace for support. They smiled.

In the peace-bringing glow of my candles, finally even fierce G.Mama Dot smiled gently. Everyone was optimistic. Starfruit and papaya and cocoplums were passed to seal the deal. It was decided. I would go to East Island *after* the OPT.

I almost asked what happened if I found out I had failed the OPT while I was in East Island. Then I stopped myself. Then I went ahead and asked.

"You won't fail," they all said at once.

In the candlelight I agreed.

We ate fruit and smiled until the smiles became yawns. Turning thirteen is exhausting for the birthday girl and her family.

Tired or not, no one shirked. Mamselle and I both helped the Godmommies wash the dishes and tidy the kitchen. When Mamselle left I kissed the Godmommies, left them drinking coffee on the porch, and went up to my room.

I want to fall asleep, except I keep thinking about that missing finger and ashes. Turning thirteen is a lot different than I thought it would be. So far some of the differences are not so good. And I'm not just talking about the second spot on my chin. I think maybe the Godmommies' quilt will help. I'm going to pull it on top of me and see.

Wishing for Sweet and Interesting Dreams,
Beebee

16

Dear Diary,

My dreams were not so interesting. That decided me: If my dreams are not going to be so interesting, I guess my life will have to be. And this being the day after tomorrow—I'm going to start my business today. And I know just what it is going to be. I'm going to start a candle company! I have even figured out the name of my company: Apies Candle Company, Incorporated. Ape means bee in Latin. I will make beeswax candles and send them out all over the world. And they won't just be everyday pretty candles—they will be peace-bringing candles.

Wax gathered from beehives on our island is very, very powerful. It creates a light that brings peace to everybody it shines on. Almost sort of like for the moments you're in the light of one of our candles, you're on the island in Bright World.

We noticed this first when a ship docked that had a crew stricken with influenza. Everybody on board was completely cranky even after we sent them lots of food. Of course they couldn't step on the island because these sail-ors were men. Rule Number One. So we could hear them fussing across the water—until we sent out a birthday cake with island candles on it. After we sent the candles out they were completely cool. After that sailors passing by always asked for candles, but we usually didn't have them so they stopped asking.

I had forgotten all about that until Mamselle and the Godmommies got to fighting and I brought the candles out and they stopped.

From all the strife and troubles I've read about in The Other World, I have to believe my candles will be a pretty big deal.

About to be busy,
BeeBee

17

Dear ignored, for just a few months, Diary,

My beezness is flying! It's so busy I haven't had time to write! The candles are getting really popular. After four months went by, Godmother Elizabethanne taught me to divide my earnings into *quarters* and how to keep books filled with everything I'd sold and earned. I couldn't make enough candles to fill all the orders we received!

That was a very good thing. Demand is higher than supply, so we get to raise prices. That is a very good thing.

I've made more money in one quarter in the candle beezness than the Godmommies make in a year in the honey business—and they've been in the honey-making business since before I came to the island. Sweet!

I said if I couldn't spend the money, I might as well start giving it away. They said that might just be the cure I needed for my brand of boredom blues. They gave me the name of a banker and an address in Switzerland and a banker and an address in the Cayman Islands. I picked the bank in Zurich. There are enough islands in my life already!

Randall and Randall Williams

I wrote to the Swiss bank. I gave them a list of the kind of things and the exact people I want to give money to—I picked out the names from what I read in the papers and magazines that arrive six months late.

Today after I sent my money and my list off I started worrying that my help would come too late, that all the problems I had read about would be solved and fixed before my money got to it. The Godmommies say I don't need to worry about that.

Problems, predicaments, and just plain pain and jams people get themselves into don't change as quick as fashion and clothes do. People in trouble six months before will still need my help six months later.

The Godmommies said the big money givers from The Other World should just look out. Me and my Swiss Bank account number are well on our way to doing some serious philanthropizing.

Baby Philanthropist is better than Baby Mogul—but I'm not sure I want to be a Baby Anything. I want to meet my first princess and start being a real teenager.

But I have to admit doing even a single afternoon of what the Godmommies call "administering my philan-thropies" does put a dent in boredom. I like making lists of what needs doing.

When I'm not administrating my philanthropies, I'm wondering about the princesses on the other side of the island or worrying about the OPT. The Godmommies tell me that I have no reason to worry about the Official

Princess Test. They're back to believing Mamselle is the very best princess coach in the whole entire world. They think they're getting more than their monies' worth.

Before Mamselle came to the island she was the head of the world's most famous princess school. My mother, Cinderella, Sleeping Beauty, Snow White, and Rapunzel were all students of hers, and all of them passed the OPT—the Official Princess Test—the very first time.

The Godmommies think the OPT is almost as bad as the ERB's and the ACT's and the SAT's. They call the OPT a necessary evil. They think the PSAT and the SAT are good reasons I'm not living in The Other World.

I want a high score on the OPT; I want to take the SAT and maybe even an ERB. Sweet as this world is, I want to be prepared for all three worlds.

Rushing to Practice Pea Sensitivity,

BeeBee

18

Dear Diary,

Even though the Godmommies and Mamselle are tight
again, the Godmommies are getting more nervous about
the OPT. And they're not nervous about what happens if I
fail it, they're nervous about what happens if I pass it. They
know if I pass it I will want to go to Raven World. I suspect
THEY WANT ME TO FAIL the OPT. I suspect I am turning into the Godmommies. I KNOW they do NOT want
me to head out for Raven World any more than they want
me to head out to the East Side of the island. I know a girl
gets to choose her own adventures.

All day they kept finding excuses or making reasons for
me not to go to Mamselle's for my final princess lessons.
And these are my final princess lessons. The Court of
Queens are on their way. They sent a bird to tell Mamselle
and Mamselle told us.

All of a sudden the Godmommies are very, very interested in my new candle company. They think I need to
expand. Immediately. They want to work with me in the

apiary. Even though the Court of Queens is expected any day.

This morning they helped me collect the wax, and they are helping me dip the wicks, and they're helping me twist the wax.

I ask the Godmommies why I have to wait to take the Princess Test before I venture off to the East Side of the island. They say, Because We Say So! And that is the end of that conversation.

We turn back to talking about the four crates of candles on the boat that's stopping on the island tomorrow. This is a big accomplishment.

When I snuggle into my bed, the leaf on my quilt looks particularly inviting. So does the throne. I wonder about the princesses on the other side of the island. The God-mommies have told me a little about them. I can't make up my mind if I would rather be friends with the girl who's a nature and adventure freak or with the girl who wants to be a queen. It's like having to choose between Huck Finn and Elizabeth the First when you want to be friends with both. I bounce back and forth, back and forth, until I'm ready to tell you all my secrets before curling in for the night.

Love,
Bizzy, Buzzy, Beebee, Mogul and (almost) Philanthropist.

19

Dear Diary,

Giant Yikes. Bad wow. Be careful what you wish for. The very last thing I wished for last night before I went to sleep was that I can do something new. Something besides the things I always do: make candles, collect honey, do yoga, swim, play chess, read books. I'm taking the OPT. TODAY! The Official Princess Test. The Queens' barge arrived just after the boat that came to pick up the candles and the mail.

Truly Terrified,
Black Bee Bright, possible Princess of Light

20

Dearest Diary, my only friend,

Today was the Princess Test. I think I flunked. Remember that book, *Alexander and the Terrible, Horrible, No Good, Very Bad Day*? Well, Diary, my day was WAY worse than his.

It started off great. The Godmommies saw the Queens' boat docked outside Mamselle's house and made me a special breakfast of "brain food"—smoked fish and a teaspoon of royal jelly. When they gave me my official OPT gown I wanted to cry.

Not long after breakfast Mamselle walked up to get me. She held my hand as we walked back to her house. For the first time ever, she talked nonstop all the way, giving me last-minute advice.

We entered her house by the back door and everything was as it has always been. Elegant. Peaceful. Quiet. Mama's picture on the wall beaming. But one thing had changed. The group pictures of all the young princesses. I could remember each name. I could tell them apart.

Today, in my princess school uniform with its black

velvet sleeves and hot and scratchy, long and heavy silver-brocade skirt, I was looking so much like each of them. I saw that. And I saw Mamselle see me see it.

When the Queens walked in wearing their very different gowns and their very different hairstyles, and their very different makeup, and their very different walks even, I couldn't believe what Mamselle had told me. Once upon a time the Queens wore the very same princess uniform as every other princess and once upon a time they had each wanted, desperately, to look exactly like the other girls. Now, each obviously wanted to look only like herself. They were a long way from the days they took the OPT and moved from belonging only to The Other World and history to being, by virtue of the OPT, fairytale, too, and immortal.

First came Sheba. I thought it was Sheba even before she spoke because she had her long emerald-colored Ethiopian gown tucked up and you could see hairy legs, and hairy legs had gotten Sheba teased by King Solomon. Sheba seemed proud of her hairy legs.

Sheba entered Mamselle's house arm-in-arm with a Chinese queen.

"Teanastellen," Sheba said, and I knew it was Sheba for sure. Sheba speaks Ge'ez. "Teanastellen" is Ge'ez.

"Selam," I said, bowing low as I tried to think of something to say to her companion.

I don't speak Chinese. When the Chinese queen said "Ni hao," I just bowed lower and hoped it was low enough to distract from my silence.

The Diary of B. B. Bright, Possible Princess

As I bowed I got a very good look at one of the red phoenixes embroidered on her gown and at one of the white
cranes. I smiled. It was the same gold hanfu decorated with
white cranes and red phoenixes that I had seen on Mamselle's
table a thousand times. When I finally rose from my bow, the
same enigmatic smile that graced Xi Wangmu's offical pho-
tograph was staring back at me. At least one of the Queens on
my court was an old student of Mamselle's. I bounced an
extra curtsy for joy. Mamselle raised an eyebrow.

That's when Hera, wearing a simple one-armed toga,
pushed herself forward, in front of Sheba, like she thought
she should have been the first one through the door from
the get-go.

Sheba glared at Hera. Then Hera, accidentally on purpose, stepped on Sheba's royal toe. Adjusting her toga,
Hera approached me with hand extended.

Since I do speak enough Greek to greet and Hera was
wearing a gown that resembled my favorite pareo, I was
excited to see her.

I was so excited I almost started to speak before she
spoke to me. That might have made me the first girl in history to fail the Official Princess Test before the greetings
were done. I stopped myself just in time.

"Gei sou," said Hera.

"Gei sas," I replied.

And then there was no time to even say anything else, as
Cleopatra, easily recognizable with those beautiful, flash-
ing black-rimmed eyes, was gliding toward me.

69

"Em hotep," said Cleopatra.

"Em hotep nefer," I responded, trying to show I spoke a little Egyptian, which is hard to do when you're also trying not to show off.

Cleopatra was followed by another dark-eyed queen, who I soon learned was Tanya.

"Vy ochen' krasivy," she said. She spoke Russian. The phrase translated to "You look very pretty." I could have said the same about Tanya. She was dressed in clothes made out of flowers and bits of forest knitted together with moss. She was very beautiful, with dark hair and eyes and pale skin. She sort of looked like Snow White or how I imagined that princess Jaz would look. Because Tanya gave me a compliment instead of a greeting I liked her immediately.

"Dorogaya, Tanya," I said, thanking her for the compliment.

Leizu, in a red kimono, was the last to enter. Placing herself between Hera and Sheba, in the tight circle that had gathered around me, she staked out her place as the peacemaker.

This time I bowed until my nose almost touched my knees. Any would-be-princess facing a court of queens knows to bow low to anyone who smells anything like kind. Leizu smelled like kindness and peace—almost like one of my candles. The scent of her encouraged me.

My court of queens complete, Mamselle shut the door. The ordeal began.

"How the mighty have fallen," said Sheba, as she turned away from me to take a good, long, slow look at the interior of Mamselle's home.

Sheba spoke in a tone of voice I had never before heard. Afterwards Mamselle told me the adjective that correctly described that tone was haughty. Whatever you call it, it made me feel small. And it made me notice, for the very first time, that the furniture in Mamselle's house was faded, torn, and stained; that much of it looked too big for her tiny house, which was built to look, from the outside, like a mini-chateau.

Mamselle stood strong. She took a deep breath. She said, "Allow me to present BeeBee. *Alors, Je m'excuse!* Black Bee . . ."

Before Mamselle could finish her sentence, Xi Wangmu leaned toward Sheba and spat, "She who *would be* Princess of Light." She announced those words in a way that made it sound like the least likely event ever to occur in the history of princess-dom.

Tanya sniffed, loudly, and cut her eyes at Xi Wangmu. I was starting to like Tanya even more.

"The very woods have already crowned her," Tanya said, reaching to pick a sprig of a wildflower from my hair. When she presented the sprig to me with a swirling motion of her hand (which Mamselle had taught me to call a flourish), I felt a new kind of royal.

"One could say unkempt," Sheba said. Hera raised her eyebrows. In a flash, all the Queens were raising and lowering their eyebrows, keeping the rest of their faces completely blank, as if talking in some secret queen code.

Cleopatra ended the silent conversation, drawling, "She does have some qualities I find interesting: she has a head for numbers, and she's willing to go adventuring in nature, sometimes alone, but she stays so much beneath the thumb of the godmothers. Perhaps too much."

With that, Cleopatra turned those giant, ringed, gray eyes right at me, like I was something she might want to eat for dinner, and purred, "What do you have to say for yourself, My Lady Contradiction?"

I bowed so low my nose almost touched the ground. I kind of bowed and curtsied at the same time. I needed time to think. I knew what I wanted to say, but I was figuring out just how to say it. Upright again, I knew.

"I am honored. The Princess Selection Committee could not have picked a more distinguished panel: the Queen of Sheba, Founder of Ethiopia, and her friend Xi Wangmu, Queen Mother of the Heavens; Cleopatra, Queen of the Nile; Hera, Queen of Olympus; Leizu, the Queen who discovered silk; and Tanya, Tsarina of the Russian Fairies. You are all beautiful, all powerful, all different. And you do not contradict what it means to be a queen. You each enhance the definition."

I had bowed after each Queen's name, then bowed one final time after my last word.

Mamselle looked like a cat that had just got the cream. I thought I might have scored my first point. Mamselle seemed to think so too.

"Perhaps now that B. B. has passed her first test we may begin in earnest," said Mamselle.

The Queens sat: Sheba plunked onto a small sofa and Xi Wangmu fluttered in beside her, flicking open and closed an elaborate fan. Tanya draped herself over and into a chaise lounge, upholstered with honeysuckle and wildflowers. Cleopatra sat a bit apart, away from the fray, on the carpet near the door. Leizu perched quite precisely on a silk chair again, situating herself between Sheba and Hera. Hera, the Queen of Olympus, sat on the tiniest footstool in the room. With her back so straight and her nose so high, Hera made the stool look like a throne.

I wasn't surprised when Sheba pronounced, "I will ask the first question."

When Hera hissed, under her breath but loud enough for everyone to hear, "Always with the questions, this queen," I controlled *most* of my laughter by putting on my Serious Princess Face.

"Silence!" said Sheba. Unfortunately Hera wasn't used to being bossed. She looked like she was about to throw something at Sheba—something like an Olympic lightning bolt! I held my breath.

Fortunately, Leizu, strong and soft as silk, stated simply, "Sheba is renowned for her questions. We agreed. Please continue, Sheba." I resumed breathing. So did everyone else. And Sheba started back with her questions.

"Why are you better than the other girls?" asked Sheba.

"I am not," I replied.

"You're not better than the other girls?" Sheba prodded.

"I am not," I said.

"This is your final answer?" asked Sheba.

"That is my answer," I said.

"And what if I were to say that if you insist on that answer you will never move from being a princess candidate to being a princess?" Sheba asked.

"It would still be my answer," I said.

This time the rivals, Sheba and Hera, came to an agreement without the aid of their peacemaker, Leizu. They huffed. Scornfully. At me. I hoped this was part of the test. I made a princessly effort to ignore them. I kept on keeping on.

"The sapphire is no better than jasper, nor jasper better than pearl, whether pink or golden. Not even the ruby is better, and padparadscha is no less. They are each perfection in their place and equal," I said.

And I thought it was a good answer. Each of the Queens was wearing her special jewel. I had my necklace around my neck. I thought it was a very good answer.

"A most original response," said Sheba. Her voice was like ice. Like being original wasn't a good thing. Like equal wasn't good. I had to suck the inside of my cheek to keep from talking back. Not being able to talk back got me mad enough to cry.

I tried not to let my chin drop down. For Mamselle and the Godmommies, I got my chin up, and my shoulders back.

I may not be a crowned princess. But I am my

Godmommies' godchild. And I am the Raven King's daughter. Even if I can't say it out loud.

I was still sucking the inside of my cheek when Leizu pulled five peaches out of the sleeve of her kimono. She wanted to get the test back on track. I could see it in the smile in her eyes.

"I like originality," said Leizu.

She placed the fruit on the table in front of me. All the peaches were beautiful but four were very, very bright peach-colored and perfectly shaped, though each a slightly different size. They were almost the same orange-pink color of the padparadscha she was wearing. One peach was pale and a bit lumpy looking.

"Choose the sweetest. Without tasting," said Leizu.

"May I touch and smell?" I asked.

"No," Xi Wangmu.

"One peach, that peach," I said pointing to the most brightly colored, largest peach, "looks sweetest. But looks can be deceiving."

I whistled. I thought five Queens were going to faint away and die right in Mamselle's house and maybe Mamselle herself was going to faint and die right along with them.

Tanya, sweet Tanya, giggled. In for a penny, in for a pound, I didn't stop whistling. Quicker than quick, my bees arrived and started swarming the light-colored and ugly peach.

I changed my whistle-tune and fireflies appeared,

distracting the bees, then leading them back out the window. I picked up the light-colored peach and offered it to Leizu.

Leizu handed the peach to Tanya, who pulled her trusty brownie knife out from her sleeve, then deftly cut each peach into six pieces.

"Insects, dirty ugly insects, are not usually invited into the palaces where princesses are found," said Hera, addressing her comment to Mamselle.

Once upon a time Hera had been Mamselle's favorite student—if the comment hurt Mamselle, she didn't let it show. I tried hard not to let my eyes or my mouth wince. But I think something showed.

The Queens each tasted a bite of the brightest peach first. One after another they made sour faces. The last queen to taste, Xi Wangmu, didn't even try the large pretty peach.

She knew from the expressions on the other Queens' faces it was bitter. And I knew, she knew, I was right. Another point, I hoped.

Next they each took nibbles of the other peaches. Finally they tasted the peach I chose. No one said a word until the last bite was swallowed.

Tanya smiled big and wide. But that was quickly forgotten. Sheba stayed in charge.

"Princesses are not beekeepers, not honey makers. And they don't whistle," said Sheba.

"I make candles. With beeswax," I replied.

"Was that an explanation, young lady?" asked Sheba.

"Not exactly," I said.

"Are you telling the complete truth?" asked Sheba.

"No, ma'am," I responded, this time with the complete truth.

"Princess Rule 416. Seldom apologize and never explain. Princess Rule 7. No useless labor. Princess Rule 3. No lying! Infraction. Infraction. Infraction!" Sheba said, almost, but not quite, shouting.

Tanya jumped in, trying to save me. "I'm sure I once apologized about something once and I'm sure I must have explained something . . . once . . ." she said, trying to defend me without telling a lie.

"I do make silk . . ." offered Leizu.

"You invented the making of silk! Did you invent the making of candles, beekeeper?" asked Sheba, pointing a finger at me.

"No, I read about it," I replied.

Even Tanya, my one friend among the Queens, seemed now confused.

"Who, darling," Tanya asked, "needs candles when we rule the moon and stars?"

All I could do was hang my head. I had given another explanation. Cleopatra got up from the floor and walked over to touch me on the shoulder. The gesture was reassuring.

Unfortunately Cleopatra's reassurance infuriated Mamselle. She thought Cleopatra was feeling sorry for me.

Randall and Randall Williams

According to Mamselle, and frequently repeated by Mamselle to me, princesses don't do pathetic. Princess Rule 17.

"Get on with it!" ordered Mamselle. For an instant the Queens were back to being potential princesses. Gazing directly into each set of eyes, the light and the dark, Mamselle silently announced that there wasn't a woman in the room who hadn't been her student. "No one," Mamselle continued aloud, "passes a test by taking half of it, not even one of you!"

For the first time that day I felt like I had something in common with the Queens: fear of our teacher. Cleopatra dropped her hand from my shoulder and took a step back before she spoke.

"We will give you a sheet of paper. You will have as much time as you need and the whole sheet to make your reply. A queen must be brave. A princess will one day be a queen. Define courage," she ordered.

Tanya produced a piece of paper. Leizu gave me a pen. I sat at Mamselle's small desk and started thinking. The Queens started getting comfortable, settling in for a long break.

Mamselle brought out a card table and some folding chairs. Hera started shuffling cards. The Queens played with a special deck, painted with Other World kings and Other World queens. The Queens started talking and gossiping about their conquests. The Jokers, Mamselle told me later, were men the Queens had loved who were not royal. Every card dealt sparked a new comment or old memory.

At each Queen's place was a stack of tokens—tiny

crowns—big enough to keep the Queens betting all evening and possibly into the morning. I should have taken this as a hint about the kind of answer they were looking for—but I didn't.

I just kept thinking about courage. And I was thinking about going to the East Side of the island. COURAGE and IMPATIENCE set in. AT ONCE. TOGETHER. I started to write. IMPETUOUS. IMPETUOUS was an old vocabulary word I couldn't understand when the Godmommies first taught it. Now, with COURAGE and IMPATIENCE telling me to get this OPT finished, I think I'm getting the GIST of it. I wanted it to be over. I wanted to finish and pass and be off to East Island. I was ready to be in the middle of the desert. Alone. I wrote faster. They were only in the second round of betting and gossiping when I lifted my arm in the air waving my exam paper.

Sheba snatched it from me.

"Three words? This is all you have to offer? Three words!" asked Sheba. Her voice was almost Godmommy-loud.

"Yes, ma'am," I replied.

"And what, pray tell, are these words?" asked Xi Wangme.

"*This* is courage," I replied, coming to my feet.

"Mon Dieu!" cried Mamselle, completely undone, this time by me.

Sheba rose. Throwing her cards face up in the center of the table, she declared, "We have seen all we need to see."

"But she hasn't had a chance to play the piano, or speak French or Spanish . . ." said Mamselle.

"We *have* seen quite enough," pronounced Leizu.

"We will let you know our decision," added Hera, adjusting her toga, before gathering her thoughts and her things to leave.

Tanya, having folded her hand quietly, was walking toward me. She touched my face.

"Skin the color of honey, lips the color of plums, and chocolate-brown eyes, " said Tanya. She spoke sadly, as if it were all either wasted or just plain arranged wrong.

My eyes were filling up with tears. I held my head down. I couldn't look at Mamselle. Looking down didn't keep me from hearing. I heard Hera fussing. She was as determined to have the last word as Sheba had been to have the first.

"Mamselle, in all of your years of preparing princess candidates, I do not believe you have ever presented a candidate such as this creature with wildflowers in her hair and wild thoughts in her head," said Hera.

"Blame me. Not the girl," pleaded Mamselle. I loved her for defending me.

Then, shocking myself as much as if I had started *talking in tongues*, I interrupted adult conversation. I spoke without being spoken to. I broke a Godmommy rule. I said what I needed to say.

"Blame me, not my teacher. I have not performed as expected. It is not that I haven't been taught. Mamselle deserves your apology. And I don't think it would make any of you less of a queen to give it to her," I said.

I took a deep cleansing breath, stood up, then waited

for lightning to strike me dead, Hera's or somebody else's. Or for another bird to drop out of the sky holding another little girl in its beak—a girl more suited to be the Princess of Light than me.

Then I walked out of the room. Without invitation or permission. I held myself in the most princessly posture I could achieve—which, at that moment, meant my hands were balled in little fists by my side and my chin was up, way up, and my shoulders way back.

They didn't wait for me to get long gone before they started talking. I could hear them as I stood just outside the door, trembling.

"For better or for worse your job here is done," said Sheba, taking back the last word.

"You will receive our decision in the usual manner," said Hera, who wouldn't let her have it.

"Mamselle is always welcome in my Kingdom," said Tanya, attempting to console her. I hated to think Mamselle needed to be consoled because something I had done injured her.

"Je suis déjà chez moi," said Mamselle simply. She was too winded even to speak in English. She was born from a French fairy tale. In the hardest times it showed. This was a hard hard time.

"No, your *home* is in a *palace*," said Leizu, blinking her eyes with such force it silenced the other queens completely and finally.

Randall and Randall Williams

"The tide awaits no one, not even six royals," said Mamselle. She was past ready to get the Queens out of her house.

Walking slowly on the path towards my bedroom in the Godmommies' cottages on the lake, I saw Sheba leading the parade to the ocean dock.

Her arm was again around Xi Wangmu. They were followed by Hera and then Cleopatra. Tanya and Leizu brought up the rear as the Queens and their chatter disappeared into the darkness and silence that enveloped East Island's dock.

I was glad to see them go. I turned and started to make my way back to Mamselle. I wanted to throw my arms around her and thank her, but I heard her before she saw me. Mamselle's words made me stop walking.

She was talking to herself in her strange French accent. Talking out loud to herself like I had actually driven her crazy.

"Enfant, when zey ask you about le courage, could not you have just told zem about ze Amazons, or Elizabeth ze first, or Oronooko, or lion mothers, or your mother for zat matter, flying you here in her beak with war blasting all around her. Flying over half ze world to get you to ze safety . . . or even you on ze leetle lake's high dive. Où, où . . ." and she was off again, in French.

I had no answer for her, Diary, and no answer for you. Nor do I have an answer for myself. I watched as Mamselle looked at the stars for a while before going back into her house—disappointed in me. I didn't move until she went back in. Then I turned and went on walking back toward the lake.

No answer except, I am who I am. And part of who I am is in a hurry. I'm writing to help me forget this day. Princess or no princess, my bees and hives need my attention.

Your Sorta-Sad,
BeeBee

21

Dear Diary,

You win some, you lose some. That's what the Godmommies said after dinner. The same tide that brought the Queens brought mail. In the mail were more fan letters for the candles, and orders and checks. And the first testimonies that my philanthropies are taking hold.

To fill the demand I am going to have to expand my apiary. I'm going to have to add more hives. I have 6,000 bees, but I need to have 12,000. I'm going to get there. I'm going to name the new queens after our recent visitors.

One day, princess or not, I want to be like the Queens. Very highly original.

Tomorrow when I tend my hives I will think about the fan letters the candles have received.

Moving on,
Beeb

22

Dear Diary,

I've got problems bigger than my coming OPT scores. My hives are starting to fail. Something's been wrong but I've been too busy with the OPT to take notice. Bees are dying and bees are not being born. I love my bees and want to take good care of them. I clean the hives, I sing to them, but more bees are dying each hour! I thought I was sad yesterday when I was down in the dumps. Now I am down below the dumps.

    I'm going to go out and move my hives to near a blackberry bush and see if that helps.

Bothered,
Bee

23

Dear Diary,

Everything's changed. Again. Turning thirteen is a lot of up and down and new information. Constantly. It feels like I'm changing too much and the world's changing too much at the very same time.

When I got in today from tending my apiaries, after dinner, the Godmommies sat around looking strange and silent. They looked like they had something they needed to say that they didn't want to say. That is not like the Godmommies. It looked like they were holding their breath. It looked like they were about to explode.

Finally, instead of exploding, each of the Godmommies put an envelope on the table. The envelopes contained letters from my mother. To me. The Godmommies were supposed to have given me the three letters with my poem on my thirteenth birthday. But they hadn't. They said they feared the letters would make me sad. They hadn't been sure I was ready. They said they had told me most of what was in them already. In bits and pieces. And dribs and drabs.

They said watching me tend my apiaries in what they called "the aftermath of your challenging experience with the Princess Test" had convinced them that I was ready to KNOW ALL that pertained to me. THAT I COULD TAKE IT. Wow.

The first letter was written the week I was born. The other two were written the day we left Ravencastle. The first letter was sweeter than sweet. The second two were very salty.

I am copying them into you, Diary, to help me memorize every word. And in case I cry over them again and blur out some of the words. I have so little from my mother. So few words, so few days, so few memories, I want to keep what little I have near always. I think I'll write these out in pencil.

Still reeling,
BeeBee

24

Dear Daughter,

Once upon a time, what will seem to you a very long time ago, while living on the East Side of Bee Isle, in my castle tower, I discovered there were Eight Princesses living on my side of the island. And me.

I call the others Sass, Ruby, Jaz, Pearl, Ammie, Tope, GiGi, and ChaCha. I have a necklace that will help you remember their names as it helped me remember their names. On the necklace is a sapphire, a ruby, a bead of jasper, a pearl, a bead of amber, a topaz, a garnet, a padparadscha, and a darkstar.

Once upon a time this necklace was mine. Only then it didn't have a darkstar dangling from its center. When the necklace belonged to me, there hung a diamond where the darkstar now rests.

The diamond symbolized my strength and my sorrow and the understanding that I had found my strength through sorrow, in tears. A diamond is hard as my resolve, clear as my truth, and the shape of the drops sprung from my eyes.

It is obvious from the hour of your birth, five short days ago, when you came into the world smiling, that you will find your strength a different way.

The Diary of B. B. Bright, Possible Princess

The darkstar is the stone I today consecrate to you as the diamond was consecrated to me.

The ruby is the stone consecrated to Ruby, and the pearl to Pearl. The sapphire is the stone consecrated to Sass, amber to Ammie, topaz to Tope, jasper to Jaz, garnet to GiGi, and padparadscha to ChaCha. I tell you this because alliances with these Eight Princesses and the necklace that will lead you to them, along with the island Bee Isle, are what I give you today, with warm hands, as your birthright.

I also give you the title Black Bee Bright, Princess of Ravencastle. The necklace is safe in a silk pouch waiting for your sixteenth birthday for you to be old enough to wear it. Wrapped up with it are my love and good wishes. And never forget you were born on the seventh day.

Love, Your Mama,
The Raven Queen

25

Dearest darling B. B.,

I write this letter in haste. As I sit at my royal desk carved of ebony wood, painted with peridot dust, glittering green, for the very last time, you are two rooms away playing with your father, the Raven King, for the very last time.

Though you are but four, today I have placed the necklace you must wear around your neck till you return to Ravencastle. Never take it off—unless you have returned to Ravencastle.

Our nation is at war. Your father's kingdom has become a very dangerous place.

We must flee. Your father inherited from his father, along with this kingdom, a magical crown made of feathers that allows a human to fly. Your father, who inherited the crown directly, requires only a single feather to fly a great distance. I, who inherit by marriage, require many feathers from the crown to fly even a short distance. Today, your father gave me all of the feathers in his crown. He loves us that much.

In a few hours I will leave with you in my arms for the small island kingdom over which I reigned as a young woman and for which you are named, Bee Isle. Nothing and no one can harm you on my island. You

90

will be safe. Everything there is, and always will be, Black Bee Bright.

I am taking you to three women I love and trust above all others. In time they will earn your love and trust as well. And in time if you cannot claim Princess of Ravencastle, mayhap you can claim Princess of Light.

To protect myself I long ago cast a magic spell on Bee Isle. No man can step foot on the island. No girl can step foot off the island until she has found the Eight Princesses. None but a royal, a princess, or a queen can enter the East Side of the island.

Your father will save the country and I will save you. It may take all his strength, all his power, and all his magic to win the battle; it may take all my strength, all my power, to fly you to safety. Or we may have enough left over to survive.

It is our hope that one day you will return to Ravencastle. It is our hope you return in our arms. But if not in our arms, with our love.

We considered going into exile as a family. We considered leaving Ravencastle to our country's enemies and all three of us fleeing to Bee Isle. In the end, we decided we could not be that selfish: our world needs you. And you will one day want and need our world. So we must save you both—if we can.

Your father and I face what comes with love and certainty as befits the old. We hope you face what comes with joy and wonder as befits the young.

Love, Mama,
Queen of Ravencastle

26

Dear, dear, Black Bee,

The current crisis has stolen my wits. There is something I almost forgot to tell you.

When the time comes, and you will know when the times comes, seek the other princesses. They are the allies who will help you reach your larger life, who will assist you in your return to Ravencastle if you must return without me and without your father. To help you find them I am leaving you the prose poem the headmistress of my princess school gave me when I moved to Bee Isle after I graduated, when I had only met Sass.

Legacy

I have just discovered I am pretty. I like to decorate my body with lovely clothes. I like to play with color on my face. I like to change the styles of my hair. The Ruby is my precious stone. I was born on Monday. I am Rubydarling.

I am always thinking, reasoning, reading. My nose is in a book. I burn with the blue light of the Sapphire. I was born on a Saturday. I am Sass.

The Diary of B. B. Bright, Possible Princess

I like to take care of puppies and kittens, and one day I want to be a mama. I am generous with my cuddles and my care. The Garnet is my precious stone. I was born on Friday. I am Gigi.

I love God and embrace mysteries. I know darkness but have returned to light. I hold the bitter past in sweet brightness. I was born on a Wednesday glowing with ancient Amber. I am Ammie.

I want to lead a city or a country. I make powerful alliances with girls and with boys. I was born on Saturday. I am Pearl.

I like to walk alone in nature. I am fiercely independent, and re-sourceful. I take excellent care of myself and shine as bright and strong as Jasper. I was born on Thursday. I am Jaz.

I revel in my senses. I like the sound of music, the feel of wind on my skin, the taste of ripe strawberry, the beauty of color, the scent of rose. I burn with the light of the Topaz. I was born on Tuesday. I am Tope.

I create paintings, and songs, and dances, and sculptures,
I am ChaCha.
I illume with the light of the Padparadscha.
I was born on Friday.
I am ChaCha.

When I was looking for the princesses it usually turned out I would find *a princess on the day she was born. That might be the same for you or it might be different. I also found sometimes it helps to let the princesses know that you're looking for them. You might want to make a flag or something to fly with their special symbols to let them know you want to meet them. When I was on the island their symbols were a heart, a book, a child in a hoop, an infinity symbol, a throne, a leaf, a rainbow palm, and a paintbrush. I will tell your godmothers all about this when we get to Bee Island.*

I hear the war bugles of our enemies getting closer. Your father has bundled you in his velvet cloak. His crown of feathers is at my feet. With God's help, he will do his part, and I will do my part, and you will do your part, and this nation will survive.

The first night of the first day you were born, I saw the darkest, most beautiful, and brightest star I have ever seen in the sky reflected in your eyes. You are beyond treasure. You are love and fortitude. You are my daughter. You are Black Bee Bright, and you are born to rule.

Love, Mama

27

Dear Diary,

The biggest, truest reason I want so much to pass the OPT is I want to be just like my mother. If I can't be like her one way I will be like her another.

Just realizing what it is to be an orphan,
Black Bee, the Raven Queen's daughter

P.S. It's kind of cool the Godmommies put the princesses' symbols on my quilt. I guess they do want me to meet the princesses even if they don't want me to go to East Island.

28

Dear Diary,

I awoke this morning with more bees dead, more hives dying, and me missing my mama. What Godmother Elizabethanne called "acute ecological distress" was crossing with what Godmommy Grace called "acute psychological distress." Leaving me to feel like what G. Mama Dot called "tore down." Looking at a postcard from a little boy who had just received a heifer from the heifer project I had contributed to, whose heifer had helped him earn money for his family; and another postcard from a girl who had been caught up in horrible bickering with her stepsiblings until they started burning my candles, made up my mind.

I am headed to the East Side of the island. I am not ready, but I am eager.

The Godmommies say knowing I am not ready but willing is a sign of the maturity I need to begin the journey.

I don't tell them how excited I am. They can see it. The idea of trekking through the desert guided only by the stars is exciting and scary. Excitement overwhelms scared when I remind myself journey's end is a land my mother loved. The place she was a young princess. This thrills me. The Godmommies gave me Rotty to protect me from the Great Pale Bear. There is only one thing standing between me and setting off: knowing what happens if the OPT result comes while I am away. I asked Mamselle, figuring she knew the most about the mechanics of the fairytale parts of the island. She said I'd be safe as long as I was a royal when I first entered.

I'm travelling light. The Godmommies give me Rotty and kisses and prayers. My quilt will be my sleeping bag. I am as prepared as I am going to be.

Almost off on an adventure,
Buzzing Black Bee

29

Dear Diary,

I have a stick that I carry three of the hives on, mainly hives
with scout bees and a few queens. I have a knapsack with my
quilt packed into it that I carry on my back. I have Zuzu,
who knows the terrain better than any, but who I fear is
much too old for this trek. Now Zuzu, who insisted on
coming along, trots beside Rotty, whom I invited. I carry a
bow and three arrows on my shoulder. G. Mama Dot
insisted on that.

    The journey began. The desert was hours and hours of
sandwalking and jitters. Every hour I thought of turning
back. Every hour I took out the map, and every time I
looked at the map, I knew I wanted to see my mother's castle. And every time I looked at my hives, I knew I had to
seek new fields for my bees. And so I kept walking. The first
night I had to sleep out in the open I couldn't sleep for
hours. I was too thrilled by the feeling of the wind on my
face. Too thrilled by the discovery the earth had provided

my food. I slept between a date palm tree and a prickly pear cactus. I got my water from the cactus and it was a sweet drink. Eventually, with my guard bees buzzing nearby, I dozed off for a few minutes, only to awake too excited to sleep or even write. Too tired to write. In the morning I walked another day. Rotty and Zuzu made stalwart companions. Tonight I sleep on the edge of the desert. We have made our way to East Island.

Expectant,
B. B.

30

Dear Diary,

This morning we hiked a steep hill. Zuzu exhausted herself leading me to a rise that allowed all three of us, Zuzu, Rotty, and me, to see, albeit from a great distance, Mama's castle tower, the big lake called Deep Pond, and East Island's dock. Far off was a speck that was probably a dolphin.

After that hard climb up and hard scramble down, Zuzu was so tired I knew I had to send her home, and I knew the only way to get Zuzu home was for Rotty to carry her. Zuzu was too tuckered to make it on her own paws. I tied my kerchief around Rotty's neck and tucked Zuzu into it. I sent them home and I told Rotty to stay home with Zuzu when they got there. It was time for me to venture alone, but I was very sad to send my four-legged companions home to West Island.

Now that Zuzu and Rotty are gone, I wish more earnestly for one of the princesses to appear. I almost felt like Gigi was standing nearby when I slipped Zuzu into the sling

100

around Rotty's neck. And just now as I write I feel the presence somewhere in the distance of Jaz. It's almost strange.

It would be too lonely without my tiny flying friends. But I have my bees and the fireflies. The fireflies have followed without invitation. I love them for it. Tonight again my guard bees will watch over me as I sleep. I love them for that. Wrapped in the Godmommies quilt I am,

Sleepy,
B. B.

31

Dear Diary,

I've entered my mother's castle. It's made of stone, three stories tall, with a turret, a balcony, and a retractable telescope, all reached by a rope ladder of dried flowers and grasses. I can't even think about my bees for the moment. This is the most beautiful place I have ever been. I don't even have heart to tell you about it. Right now everything I'm seeing is just for me to know.

Love,
Black Bee Bright

32

Dear Diary,

I have found my mother's diaries. They were laying atop
her hope chest. I am rich beyond my imagination.

Blessed
BeeBee

33

Dear Diary,

The pages of Mama's diaries are so dry and crackling apart I am going to copy my favorite entries before they turn to dust and blow away.

TALE OF A SAD PRINCESS

Once upon a time, a very long time ago, there was a sad princess with no father and a mean mother who hurt her daughter. The daughter ran away to princess school.

After the Sad Princess graduated from princess school, she planned to move to an island and build herself a fortress tower where she could work as an astronomer and hide away from the world—particularly her cruel mother.

The Sad Princess searched the world and found the most beautiful island, which wasn't on many maps. On this island she built a tower. The walls of this tower were very, very high and very, very strong. Its bricks were made from the dirt of her own land, baked in a kiln of her own creation. She placed each brick herself. The tower became her castle.

The Diary of B. B. Bright, Possible Princess

She furnished her castle with treasures from the corners of The Other World: seashells from the bottom of the deepest, most color-filled ocean, dandelions from a vacant lot, snowflakes from the arctic circle, volcanic sand from a dark and distant shore, and perfumed whispers of the eastern winds. Then she stopped traveling.

The princess had become a queen.

On the top floor of the castle the queen built an observatory. She installed a telescope. Sleeping during the day, studying the stars at night, she taught herself to be an astronomer.

The maps she drew of the sky were picked up once a year by a boat that took them to The Other World, where they became highly prized.

Year after year, sky after sky, she moved back and forth between the powerful telescope and the little bed on which she slept. Year after year, she watched the changing yet constant sky while inhabiting the changing but inconstant earth.

The cold, distant, and brilliant stars were her only friends.

Eventually a family of mice and a shih tzu who had jumped ship began to frequent the castle grounds. Every morning, before she fell asleep, the queen would groom the dog, whom she began to call Zuzu, groom her, and tie a new ribbon in her topknot.

Every night when the princess awoke, the dog would have returned from her adventures missing her ribbon. At midnight the queen would feast, feeding the mice tiny morsels from her plate. Such were their upside-down days.

Winter blew into the tropics one year. This was an occasion so rare the queen was unprepared. She ran out of firewood. Then she ran out of furniture, dresses, and bric-a-brac to feed the flame that *kept her from freezing. She turned to her bookshelves, determined to choose a volume with which she could part. But cold as she was, she could not, would not, burn a book.*

Instead, she burned the stairs, tread by tread, from the cellar to the observatory, hoping for spring's arrival, which did not happen until her staircase was entirely gone.

The queen never left the observatory now. That year when the boat came to pick up her maps, she didn't go down to the boat dock. The boat never came again. From that day on, she received no visitors—except the stars, who needed no stairs.

One night the queen was gazing into the heavens when a raven appeared and began circling above her. The queen was hypnotized by the circles in which the bird flew. The raven came so close the queen could see the purple and green threads running through his black marble beak. The queen could see her own face in his eye. Poof! The raven vanished. That night the stars seemed only cold and distant and not so brilliant after all.

The next morning the queen had new treasures to add to her wealth. Her tears had turned to diamonds on her pillow. When the sun fell upon the jewels a rainbow splashed across the walls of the queen's observatory.

That night the queen's hands were trembling when she began to search the sky for the raven with her telescope. Gazing into the luminous dark calmed her. She discovered the bird gazing down upon her royal self, across the distance, with powerful eyes that needed no instrument. Just as she saw the bird, it plunged toward her.

Bravely, the queen extended her lovely, honey-colored hand. The black bird landed. Touching her skin, he dazzled the queen with a flash of light.

When she could see again, she blinked her ebony eyes. Before her stood not a raven but a king.

Randall and Randall Williams

"Who are you?" asked the queen. The king was so much in awe of the queen's beauty he didn't know what to say, so he said something rather silly.

"I am a seeker of truths and an asker of questions," said the king. "I look for the rhythms that permeate chaos."

The queen was rather uncertain as to what he meant by all that. She frowned. The king continued talking.

"There is a harmony in you that I do not comprehend, the existence of which I question. Nonetheless, your beauty is undeniable. Your beauty is certain. I have searched the universe for a simple truth. And now I have found it," said the king.

"My beauty?" asked the queen.

"Your beauty. It is the one certain thing I have found in this universe," said the king. The queen laughed. The king frowned. He was intent on being serious.

"Allow me to do you a service," offered the king.

"Can you make the stars less distant?" asked the queen of the shining king. "I have seen you flying with them."

"If you sing into my ear, and hold my hand, I will carry you upon my wing, to all the stars, even the most distant. And I will carry you to Ravencastle."

"What is Ravencastle?" asked the queen, who had been the Sad Princess.

"A place where you will be happy," said the Raven King.

And for a long time they lived happily ever after.

The End

And that's how Mama met Daddy and the Sad Princess became the Raven Queen. It's funny to think about Mama before she had me.

Ever after,
BeeBee

34

Dear Diary,

Last night after copying out Mama's story I dreamed that
Princess ChaCha was with me. After that, I dreamed that I
read the Godmommies Mama's story and they were hugging me and tears were in their eyes. G.Mama Dot said,
"You've got to find a way or make a way. Like your Mama
did." Dreams are strange.

The more I think about it the more I think the Godmommies have already met the Princesses. Maybe before
they came to the island. I think G.Mama Dot knows Cha-
Cha. Godmother Elizabethanne knows Sass, Godmommy
Grace knows Ammie, and they all know Gigi. And I think
the Godmommies are every bit as original as the Queens.

Love,
The Raven Queen's daughter, Black Bee Bright

35

Dear Diary,

Three hours ago, I found the most perfect field for my bees. I was just beginning to hang the first of three hives I brought from West Island up in an East Island tree when the notorious Great Pale Bear, GPB, stomped into my camp and headed straight for my biggest hive, which was, unfortunately, resting on the ground, ready for cleaning.

I threw a rock, behind the bear, away from me and my bees. GPB started growling and moving toward me, fast.

I couldn't believe it. I got that rock trick from a book. A big, thick, authoritative book on bears that said bears run toward the sound of a falling rock. Good thing I didn't read just one bear book. When GPB started charging I switched to an alternative strategy.

I held my hands up over my head, hoping it made me look a foot and a half taller, and started screaming and running straight at the bear. I don't know if GPB thought I was too big to fight, or too crazy to fight—but he took off.

I read the part about the hands and arms in a book. The

part about screaming and running straight at him I made up myself. Some situations holler back for improvisation.

I tied the hive high up in a tree. I checked my bees. They were good and getting better. I could already see it. With new fields, new flowers, and new water, they were back to their old dances, the ones they had forgotten. My bees were zipping and zapping around, drawing the patterns in the air that organized their work and the patterns that attracted new bees to the hives. The particular buzz that means the work is going good was loud in my ears—for the first time in weeks their dances looked sober.

Tonight I will fall asleep exhausted.

Love,
Tuckered B. B.

36

Dear Diary,

Wrong again! When I got back to castle tower after hanging up the hive, I found a baby bird that had fallen from its nest and onto the path leading to my front door.

I was careful not to touch her with my fingers. I picked her up with leaves and returned her to the nest, where I found three other baby birds and fragments of the four eggshells out of which they had emerged. I hoped maybe their mother was out hunting for worms or grubs to feed them. They chirped so plaintively. (That was a vocabulary word months ago, but I didn't know what it really meant until I heard those baby birds chirp.) I thought my heart would break. A moment later, I saw a small wildcat padding off with what looked like a mama bird in its mouth.

There was nothing to do but pick up the nest and carry the baby birds in with me. I carried the nest very gingerly. I sang back to the birds to try to make them feel less alone. I didn't know if it was being carried, or my singing, or the warmth of my hands, or the comparative comfort of Castle Tower, but the baby birds' chirping started sounding less plaintive and more cheerful. Hearing my birds' more cheerful songs was better than taking a nap.

With my little bit of working rest, my mind cleared, and it occurred to me my birds were either hungry or soon to be hungry. I tucked them in a safe corner of my mama's bedroom vanity and started rummaging through her bookshelves looking for a bird book.

I found a few. I found a giant book by some man named Audubon with beautiful pictures of birds, but that book had nothing to say about how to feed birds, and one called *Byways and Bird Notes* by one Mr. Maurice Thompson. I found one that might have been truly helpful—if it were not so long—called *A Systematic Classification of Birds of the World* (whew, even the title is a mouthful!) by Frank Alexander Wetmore. I found a cool but impractical book called *Firebirds and Rocs, Flights of Myth and Imagination*. And then, just as I was about to give up on the books and just (forgive the pun) wing it, I found a book written by my mother, *The Birds of Bee Isle*.

Turning quickly to the chapter on baby birds, I saw my mama had divided the baby birds' section between nestlings, or newborns, and fledglings, or little ones able to leave the nest for a little while, but still pretty attached to their own mamas. And I saw a lot of warnings. There was a warning that most baby birds that looked like they were abandoned weren't. Well, I knew mine were abandoned because I saw the mama bird being carried off limp in a cat's mouth. And there was a warning that it wasn't true a mama bird wouldn't accept a baby bird back into the nest after it was touched by humans. And then there was a warning against feeding baby birds regular worms in case some of them have parasites. After all the warnings there were drawings of the island birds as nestlings and fledglings.

I found a picture that looked like the birds I had found. I discovered my birds could be fed raisins and waxworms. Finally a bit of useful information— thanks, Mama! I knew exactly where to get both!

I also discovered I was very, very lucky. Some baby birds need to be fed every forty minutes. Some every two hours. But my birds only needed to be fed every three hours, because the waxworms of Bee Isle are especially nutritive!

I went down to my hives and searched the combs for waxworms. I found enough for a snack for all four nestlings. I went to my knapsack and retrieved enough raisins for my nestlings to feast on till they could fly which, according to the number of feathers they had and the amount they were eating, would be anywhere from two to six days. I could handle a week of being Bird Mama.

When I finally fell asleep I had a dream about a movie the Godmommies acted out to me called *Fly Away Home*, about a girl who teaches a flock of wild geese how to fly by flying ahead of them in a plane.

I woke up in the middle of the night to feed my nestlings more raisins. I had learned from Mama's book there are three holes in a bird's mouth: one in the middle of the tongue, one in the roof of the mouth, and one at the back. That's where I am careful to put the raisins.

It's hard being careful in the middle of the night when you're sleepy. But I feed them using the dropper part of one of my mother's old perfume bottles as a spear. Her vanity is now a bird nursery. Every bite I offer I worry that I am putting in the wrong place, but I trust my nestlings' instincts to gobble right, and they do. And I do trust myself to be careful enough. I am a proud mama when all their hungry chirping turns to content silence.

My nestlings full, I walked down to check on my bees, missing Zuzu and Rotty, but happy to be walking under the moon alone. The hives are quiet but not silent. There is a healthy sleeping hum. The temperature of the air is almost exactly the temperature of my skin. There's a breeze. On this side of the island the breeze carries the scent of flowers I don't know the names of and in the darkness I cannot see. I breathe more deeply to let these new fragrances in and, with them, the unseen colors. My body goes all-over shivery.

On the West Side of the island I am never alone out in the dark long enough to notice the strong scent of night flowers. I know the flowers by day when it is their colors and shapes that register loudest and strongest. Or maybe I notice the smell sometimes, when or if I ever bother to push my nose into the center of a flower.

Many's the time G.Mama Dot has said, wiggling one of her short, beautiful, fat fingers at me, "You've got to stop and smell the roses, child." Many's the time I have done that in obedience. Tonight the flowers stopped me.

Tonight I did not stick my nose into flower petals; flower scent, roses and orchids and primroses and lilies and lotus, floated in through my mouth and my nose, flowed deep into my chest—like just breathing was a yoga position and air was the best dessert ever.

I tried to imagine what it felt like to be Eve her first day in Eden. I wondered if she felt just like me as she wandered through her garden away from Adam. Then I stopped mind wondering, and went body wandering.

Walking calms me. Exhaustion evaporated as I inhaled the scent of flowers and left my body, wordlessly shimmering with the joy of being a person on the planet beneath a full moon in flower-scented air.

It was as if the universe was spritzing me as I walked and breathed with reviving perfume. The colors I could see in the moonlight were the prettiest colors ever.

I picked up a stone from the ground. Aiming carefully, I threw it at the slender branch holding a bunch of grapes. The bunch fell through the air and into my hands. I washed the grapes in the flowing stream, then I ate them sitting on my high rock—they still had the sweetness of all the day's sun. For the first time I noticed the slick softness of their skin and the pure fun of spitting seeds.

It was a very good day. Sitting on the rock I felt the presence of Tope. When I closed my eyes I could see her sitting with me. A strawberry in her hand, a topaz 'round her neck, telling me there was no better princess than a princess who loved the pleasure of her five senses, a princess who responds to nature's taste, sight, sound, touch, and scent.

Beneath that moon, I agreed with Tope. I opened my eyes. She vanished. Of course she vanished; I had imagined her. But maybe she had been there. When I opened my eyes, I noticed wild strawberries growing out of the rock that I had not noticed before. I picked one and put it in my mouth. I called out loud in case she could hear me, "TOPE!" Beneath that moon, in a wind I could taste and feel and see and smell, I thought Tope was the most fortunate of the Princesses. I hugged myself as I shivered. I had just remembered it was Tuesday.

Back in my mother's room, looking at my baby birds sleeping, still, full, and fed from my hand, I thought perhaps it is Gigi who is most lucky. Or even Jaz.

I wish Jaz would show herself clearly. Once or twice I thought I'd seen her when I was crossing the desert. I feel Jaz walking with me when I walk beneath the moon, beneath the leaves so far from home. If I had not discovered that joy I would never have felt the shivering shimmer of my skin beneath the moon or the warmth in my tummy from taking care of my nestlings. It makes sense that Jaz does not show herself. As I imagine her she is Miss Independence. Like Me. Like the new Me.

Love,
Independent B. B.

37

Dear Diary,

I woke up this morning, fed the birds, then ran out to check my hives. Again. Wax is taking shape and honey is flowing. The queens have their workers inspired!

It looks like the air and water of the East Side of the island is as good for the bees as it is for me. I taste a bit of the honey and I know for sure. It is sweeter than sweet. When I return to the West Side of the island I will lead a larger swarm from my West Side apiaries to the East Side of the island. Probably more than one.

Between hive work and lunch, I spent time in my mother's library trying to figure out what the problem must be with the West Island ecology. And how I might fix it.

Best I can figure, the most likely culprit is some kind of toxic dumping going on that is affecting the West Side of the island but isn't affecting East Island due to the wind and tide patterns. Best I can figure.

If Godmommy Grace were here she would say, "Environmental racism is a big problem." G. Mama Dot would say, "It figures the royal side of the island would be the side of the island furthest away from environmental stress. Rich folk protect themselves." I say I want the whole world to be like the East Side of the island was last night. Earthy. Clean. Deep-Breath Inspiring and Providing. I'm going to sell enough candles and fund enough philanthropies to help that happen.

After lunch. But first I have to feed my birds again. Reading time goes by so fast. For a moment, when I was in the library, I looked up real quick and I thought I could see Sass. Then, who, or what, I thought I saw disappeared. Is it possible to meet someone you can't see? I almost think so. And I think I just met Sass. Wow. Good Wow!

Your very hungry, slightly sassy, trying not to blink,
Black Bee Bright

38

Dear Diary,

After lunch, my lunch and my birds' lunch, I decided I would spend the afternoon drawing a picture of Tower Castle because a Tower Castle picture would make a perfect souvenir for the Godmommies. And because I have realized Tower Castle was the place my mother predicted she would live happily ever after even before she was living happily ever after. But first I had to find some art supplies.

Mama's room was full of books and bookshelves, but I hadn't yet found any paints or pencils. This had surprised me because Mamselle had often told me my mother was a gifted painter, and I had seen examples of her work hanging in all three of the Godmommies' houses and in Mamselle's house. I was about to give up when I thought of poking into the way back deep of her overfull but still neat closet. In the way back deep I found colorful gowns, a mirror and a window, a tennis racket and some roller skates, but no canvasses or paints or colored pencils, or secret compartments. I shut the closet door, disappointed.

Randall and Randall Williams

Deciding to make do with plain pencils, ink, and paper, I spread myself in the middle of the room in front of the fireplace and began to draw the fireplace, all the gewgaws on it, and the painting above it, as a kind of warm-up.

The painting was of a huge pink rose, hanging in a blue sky just where you would expect the sun to be. The title tag was written in perfect princess calligraphy and read, "Expect the unexpected." The petals were a pink that was almost salmony red. When I looked at the painting, with my right ear almost on my right shoulder, the rose looked almost purple. If I looked at it with my left ear on my left shoulder, it looked an orangy red. The color was magical. So magical I really wished I had some paints. I wanted to paint a shade-shifting pink all of my own. I stared at the painting to remember it. Scribbled in the corner, almost so small I couldn't see it, was my mother's signature. Now I really, really wished I had some paints. Since I didn't, I drew some of my petals shaded dark gray and some of them shaded light gray, and some of them not shaded at all. My flower was pretty. My flower was sweet. My flower was not colorful. And my flower was not as pretty as my mama's flower.

I decided maybe it was because I had made my flower too small. I selected a clean piece of white paper. I drew a rose almost as big as my head. Then I drew a rose the size of my palm. I laughed. It was a picture of Mama and me. Mama's painting had inspired me. Again. Hope returned. And I knew just where to look for Mama's art supplies!

The Hope Chest at the bottom of her bed! Mama's

should be empty because she was married, and a Hope Chest is supposed to hold all the things you need when you marry and start a new life—things like sheets and blankets. However, expecting the unexpected, I dashed toward Mama's Hope Chest and lifted the lid. It was full of watercolors, and colored pencils, oil paints in tubes, modeling clay, collections of jars of colored beads, and colored yarns and silk threads. There was even a small tambourine and a tiny reed flute. Mama's Hope Chest was a treasure trove.

And not just any treasure trove. A treasure trove filled with things I needed to create art. Beautiful sounds and beautiful pictures. I giggled at my good fortune. Then I helped myself to all the colored pencils, some of the tins of watercolor, a palette, and many brushes. Before it was time to feed my birds again, I had created a sketch of Tower Castle with the telescope out and a sketch of Tower Castle with the telescope in, and I had watercolored in my sketches to bring them to life—even if they were buildings.

After the next nestling feeding I walked down to the creek with just my watercolors, brushes, and papers and painted a picture of my rock. My rock is the rock I had sat on beneath the stars, serenaded by night birds, drinking in the sweet scents of barely seen flowers, in what I was coming to think of as my moon garden.

When I was finished with those three, I went back to my mama's bedroom and drew my nestlings. It was hard getting them to sit still, but I didn't want to ever forget them, and they would be flying off soon.

Finally, I stuck my canvasses to the mantelpiece with dabs of honey in the top two corners. I loved these pictures. I had always loved to paint and painted pages of mine had often littered the big table in the Godmommies' kitchen and covered the Godmommies' walls, but these paintings were different.

Those paintings were of what I saw. These were paintings of what I *felt* when I saw. Big difference.

I could see it brightest in my rock painting. I had begun it by painting lines. I had begun it by painting the scene before me: daylight, sun, and vivid flowers. I wasn't halfway through before I realized that wasn't the painting I wanted to be painting.

I changed and started trying to draw something with no lines to it, the scent of the night. Intangible. Another vocabulary word it had taken me until JUST NOW to understand. Before long the sun had become a moon and many things once clearly visible were now obscured—and somehow the scent of the night and even, maybe, the colors inside me when sitting on the rock, colors which had been obscured, became clearly visible.

Everything that had been different since my thirteenth birthday that I couldn't find words to tell, I found colors to show. As I painted, what began as a sketch of the rock quickly turned into a picture of me right in this very moment, in Mama's castle with her paints, without me being in it at all.

As a kind of joke, off to the side and barely visible, I

painted ChaCha as I imagined her. Unlike Jaz, I didn't have a feeling that I had caught a glimpse of ChaCha on the island. But I had had some strange sense that she had guided my brush as I painted. Her face was in every light and every shadow of my pictures. My East Island sketches were the best!

I decided to paint a picture of ChaCha, but I ended up with a picture of me. The best painting of me I have ever done. If this is ChaCha, she could be my twin!

It was time for me to go feed the birds. Again. Time for me to wash and dress and feed myself supper. I thought of the old ethical puzzle I had heard Godmother Elizabeth-anne pose, "If you were fleeing a burning building and could only save an artist's dog or his amazing painting, which would you choose?"

I still have to choose the dog, but now I'm sorrier about it.

Brush Brandishing Bright,
Artiste!

P.S. G.Mama Dot always said she would save the painting. I didn't use to understand that. Now I do.

39

Dear Diary,

My bees are doing so well on this part of the island they barely need tending. When I worked on the hives today I noticed that queens, worker bees, drones, nurses, and scouts were all busy establishing new hives.

The hive is an interesting place. They feed the new to-be queens royal jelly to help them grow large and queenly. They take excellent care of those might-be-queens.

The hive takes almost as good care of the might-be-queens as the Godmommies took care of this might-be-princess.

But when there is an old queen who can't do her job, the other bees get really close to her until she is surrounded and her body temperature rises and she dies in all that live-love warm.

The Godmommies and the beekeeping books call this balling. I hate balling, but didn't know that till today. Till today I had never seen it. I had only heard about it. It's different to see it.

I love my bees. I love the wax and the honey. I like

126

their hard work. I love the waggle dance, the tremble dance, the flower-hop humming dance. I love the way they pamper the queens. I hate the balling, but it's all part of a healthy hive.

I saw that today. I mean literally, truly, actually saw it. And I mean figured it out. There are things in life I don't and won't like but which I guess must be natural and necessary. When I was on the West Side of the island the Godmommies kept those things away from me.

You can't take the best care of a hive unless you know all of what goes on in a hive. Funny, before leading this swarm I didn't really take care of the hives, I just got to take some of the wax from the hives, and I got to boil it and purify it. I got to see the busy-ness of my bees, and taste the sweet flavor, but I didn't see the sad parts of their story. I didn't see the parts that make you stop and wonder and worry.

I've been doing a lot of wondering and worrying on the East Side of this island. When I fed the waxworms to my baby birds, I was glad they were the kind of baby birds who eat insects and fruit and not the kind that eat little furry or fluffy animals. I wouldn't have liked to have had to feed them baby mice. I am truly thankful my bees are flowertarians. They just eat flower nectar.

The Godmommies told me a story about a girl in the countryside, I think it was in Tennessee, who killed lightning bugs. Well, she called them lightning bugs, but I call them fireflies. Anyway, this Tennessee girl powdered her face with firefly bodies to make her eyelids and her lips shimmer and shine with stolen brightness in the starry night.

I could not *not* kill an insect to steal its light. But I have swatted a mosquito. I have slapped one after it bit me and seen the blood on my leg. On this side of the island I worry and wonder about things like that.

Right now I'm puzzling why it's all right to feed a wax-worm to a starving baby bird and not all right to smash a lightning bug to make makeup.

Since I turned thirteen I've found myself thinking on puzzles like this. Not every day but sometimes. Periodically. Even before I got to East Island. In the amber light of this, the afternoon the queen in my hive died, I go over these puzzles over and over. Like why is there a tiny spider trapped in the amber bead that hangs on my necklace? Why is there a bit of death in something so beautiful? How can it be beautiful if there is that bit of death in it? If I met Princess Ammie, I believe she would know.

Godmommy Grace told me amber is so ancient, sometimes you get a piece with a thousand-year-old insect trapped in it. I'm not sure that explains enough. I'm sober and sorry one of the queens in one of my hives died today and even sorrier that she was killed.

Bewitched and Bothered,
BeeBee

40

Dear Diary,

Last night I read myself to sleep. I read *The Tempest*, written by Mr. William Shakespeare. I would want Miranda to be my best friend, except I want to steal Ferdinand from her, except (no hard feelings, Shakespeare!) I wouldn't want his name to be Ferdinand. Yikes.

Miranda is a lot like me. But not exactly like me. She lives on a magical island with her father and a lot of books and a crazy servant called Caliban. She and her father have political enemies. That's why they're on the island. Then one day a boat comes with a beautiful prince. And Miranda gets to go back home. WITH THE PRINCE. So unfair. I am GREEN with jealousy. But I am also happy.

It's funny how far a book can go to take your mind off what the Godmommies call "all the troubles of the world."

Randall and Randall Williams

I never noticed many of the troubles of the world until I started to be in charge of a few things. Now that I'm thirteen I am noticing many of the troubles of the world. I guess it comes with being in charge of a few things. Including me. And I'm even noticing some little troubles in me. Places I plain contradict myself.

I am starting to suspect it's easier to work on the troubles of the world—move hives, philanthropize—than it is to work on the contradictions of me.

All of that disappears when I'm reading. Or, it reappears in a way that I'm comfortable with. Like Walt Whitman. Mama had a page turned down in a book, one where he says, "Do I contradict myself? Well then, I contradict myself. I am large. I contain multitudes." I mean, what a relief! I guess I can go on ahead and contain multitudes too! Or here—what I like about Mr. Shakespeare's plays—symmetry: all over the place stuff matches. Two sets of friends meet two sets of friends. There's always five acts in a play. There's always fourteen lines in a sonnet. Everything is always rhyming.

Knowing what to expect is what I love about math, too. Two plus two equals four every day of the week. And a single side of an equilateral triangle the perimeter of which is 9 will always be 3. Math is restful.

Shakespeare is restful. The world of books, math, fiction, poetry, and biographies are a great big vacation from all the hot, hard uphills and whiplash-fast downhills of real and messy life.

I've got to get back and find out how and if Miranda gets off *her* island.

Love,
Black Bee, reader, writer, ever Brighter

41

Dear Diary,

I found out more than how Miranda got off her island!
There was a letter from Mama tucked between the last pages
of *The Tempest.*

Dear, dear Black Bee,

*If you are reading this letter you are old enough to come to the
East Island and you are the girl I imagined you would be, one who
would find and read my copy of* The Tempest.

*I apologize for the Godmommies lying and telling you there was
a bear cave and a snake pit on this side of the island. That was my
idea. I didn't want you to see Tower Castle till you were old enough
to appreciate all its treasures—just the way I will leave them for you.*

*If you are thirteen, and I don't imagine you will find your way to
this side of the island long before or long after you turn thirteen
(Happy Birthday, Darling)—if you are thirteen, you have cried long
and hard for me and for your father.*

The Diary of B. B. Bright, Possible Princess

With love and time, even seasons of deepest mourning end. If I know the Godmommies and Mamselle, you have been loved. And there has been time. Please allow East Island to be for you what it was for me—a sacred place of new beginning.

I write this letter imagining my daughter dancing, my daughter rejoicing. That is why I put the little tambourine in my hope chest. My last triumph is imagining your future delight. Never steal my last triumph from me.

Love, Mama

Mama expected me. She knew just where I would land, all these years away. And she did send Mamselle. I am the happiest girl in the world, and I'm going to fall asleep with Mama's tambourine in my hands. And my story quilt wrapped around me tight.

Soon to be,
The Raven Queen's dancing, snoozing daughter

42

Dear Diary,

Today a tropical storm hit this side of the island. It was raining too hard for me to leave Tower Castle. I spent the day feeding the birds and poking through my mama's closet.

Her closet is packed with the most wonderful gowns! A palette of colors, shimmering and shiny, splashed across the wall when I opened the door. I decided to try one on. I stood and looked at myself in the mirror. I didn't look like me. I looked pretty. To me.

The Godmommies always say I'm pretty and I believed them up until I was about ten. Or maybe it was about eight. When I was eight or ten I started not believing. I started to worry and wonder if other girls would think I was pretty.

I didn't think they would. From what I could see in West Island mirrors, I didn't look that much like the girls I saw in magazines. I squinted. I posed. I sucked in my cheeks. I lifted my chin. I stuck out my tongue. I still wasn't as pretty as those magazine girls.

The Diary of B. B. Bright, Possible Princess

The Godmommies said those magazine girls weren't as pretty as those magazine girls. They say that photographers brushed the air or some crazy thing, to make them look "like a fool idea of everybody-look-one-kind-of-way pretty" or they Photoshopped them. The way they said it, Photoshopped rhymed with head-cut-off. Ba-ad news.

If the Godmommies didn't think it essential to my future safety (in case we ever have to travel incognito to, or through, The Other World, *if* I ever meet The Eight Princesses, and *if* I ever get to step foot off the island, for me to be familiar with the habits and the styles of Other World girls), they wouldn't even let me read those swishy magazines.

The Godmommies told me over and over my mama was one of the great beauties of her time. They said I look just like her. But I don't. I've seen pictures of Mama when she was my age—and I don't look exactly like her. Mama was prettier than the girls in the magazines. Mama was beautiful. I am not Mama Pretty, or Cinderella Pretty. Or Godmommy beautiful. I'm boring. Plain. Me.

Till today. Today, I made friends with the mirror. Standing before the silver-backed glass, first in my mama's dress, looking at myself like I've never looked at me before, then in just my skin, I looked just exactly like myself and just exactly like I was supposed to. Absolutely pretty enough.

Pretty enough to enjoy adornment and ornament. Wow. Good Wow. I step into another of my mama's gowns. I have found a new way of playing with color—trying on my mother's clothes. And painting my face!

Randall and Randall Williams

I wasn't up to killing any of my lightning bugs and I didn't have to—I had the remainder of my fruit salad. I painted my eyelids with a mix-mash of blueberries and blackberries, and colored my lips with raspberries. I didn't need to add any color to my cheeks; all this sleep and East Side island air and sun had me brown and shiny. I pulled my hair tight into a puffball, then I put it into braids, then I put it in a bun, then I let it fall down on its own just like it wanted to fall, into crispy curls.

Usually before this, every way I did my hair I didn't like it. Today every way I did my hair I *did* like it. And it was fun to choose what way I liked it *best*. One of the funny things that made me look absolutely truly beautiful was that there were three or four butterflies that insisted on landing on my head and fluttering just where a big silk bow or some beads might be. The butterflies were being so sweet to me I decided then and there I needed to be sweeter to myself. I'm going to stop poking at my spots and biting my fingernails.

I completely undressed before I changed back into my regular pareo. My body is starting to change. I have curves. Little bitty ones, but definitely ones. And I'm not as skinny as I used to be, but I have decided to be fine with that. Not one thing on this island has made me think there is only one kind of way to be just right.

I put on another of my mother's dresses, then another. I sat at my mother's vanity table and hairpinned new flowers into my hair. Mama's silk flowers. I looked like a princess in a fairytale book. I stared into the mirror to see my handiwork. I touched my fingertips to the fingertips of my reflection. It was a silly thing to do and I only did it once and I will only confess it to you but I kissed myself in the mirror!

Silly, silly,
B. B.

43

Dear Diary,

A BOY IS ON THE ISLAND. I met a boy! And he hasn't disappeared—at least not yet. And he may be the hottest, coolest boy in the history of the world! Unfortunately, he acts like he knows it.

Stuck in the middle of a magic island, I met a so-oo-oo cute boy. If I hadn't read *The Tempest* I would be surprised.

Thank goodness for behinds, buckshot, and Tennessee relations. If it wasn't for them, Chance (his name is Chance) might be dead! Already.

I will never, ever, ever again fail to pay attention to any of the Godmommies' stories about distant cousins. I will hang on every word. But I'm getting ahead of myself.

So, it all started with that crazy bear coming back for my hives again. You know, Diary, the one I did the BeeBee screaming running crazy show for? Yeah, I scared him off, *again.* I contemplated a more dramatic action than just scaring him off—I got out my bow. I didn't do anything with it, but I sure got ready.

Then I settled into lunch. I gathered some lettuces, watercress, and scallions from a creek bed, and was just picking wild strawberries when I heard something about six feet tall moving toward me through the underbrush—and I just knew the Great Pale Bear was back.

I had walked over twenty miles, I had found bee paradise, and it had *attacked*. Once, about to be twice. I was hungry, I had released my nestlings-now-fledglings into the world, and I was already missing them. I was not at my Black Bee brightest.

I invoked lethal weapons. I ordered my guard bees to attack—and to go straight for the eyes and the nose—without first getting a clear look at my target.

I knew better. Hearing the butts and buckshot story is how I even know what buckshot—ammunition deer hunters use—is. Two cousins went hunting; both shot at *movement* in the underbrush instead of a deer they could *clearly see*—and both ended up with buckshot in their behinds! I guess everybody takes a turn acting "past foolish."

If you want to see my turn acting a fool, look in God-mommy slang dictionary under the phrase *past foolish*. You'll see a picture of Yours Truly in the most perfect bee field screaming "attack!" a moment before I spin around to see, not the Great Pale Bear, but a gorgeous brown boy on a beautiful black horse and my bees headed straight at his eyes.

The next word out of my mouth was *"Eek!"* Unfortunately my bees don't know that word. Just in time, I did manage to croak out, "Stop!"

139

Randall and Randall Williams

"Stop" is a very good word to say when your bees are headed straight for a boy the Godmommies would say looks better than brown on sugar. A boy as beautiful as that on a handsome horse is not something this girl wants to see her bees stinging. Fortunately, my bees are genius at changing direction.

"Attack?" the young stranger screamed back at me, ignoring my "stop" command.

"I thought you were a Great Pale Bear," I said, trying to explain.

"A polar bear on a tropical island?" asked the gorgeous stranger. And he didn't just ask the question, he smirked at me—like I was the dustiest, silliest thing he had ever seen. Like I looked ridiculous wrapped in a piece of cloth. And he was looking so fine—in his fancy silk brocade riding breeches. At least I was wearing my best travel pareo.

I was too busy trying to decide if he was mostly cute or mostly his own biggest fan, to wonder why it was he hadn't disappeared (Big Rule Number Two, you know, Diary). But I sure as shootin' wasn't too busy to let him know he didn't know everything.

"Not a polar bear, an ash-colored brown bear," I said. He looked around and raised his eyebrows. He just knew that I was lying, just knew I had made up the Great Pale Bear, knew that there was no bear at all. WHATEVER! I'd like to see his face when he actually does run into the GPB, Diary. I really really would.

I was busy figuring out that the speck Rotty and Zuzu and I had seen from the rise was probably this stranger's boat. I was also figuring out why the stranger hadn't disappeared. I was thinking it was most probably because he hadn't stepped foot onto the island. Maybe he had ridden off his boat and onto the island on his horse's back. Maybe the horse had stepped four hooves onto the island, but the stranger had yet to step a foot.

I was coming to that conclusion almost exactly at the same moment the rider dismounted his horse. He started walking toward me with that same goofy smirk on his face— before I could warn him not to. I winced. He did not disappear. He got close enough to offer me his hand to shake. He bowed low. He still hadn't disappeared.

"Prince Chance, at your service." He extended his hand. I offered mine, my wince turning into a frown.

"You shouldn't have gotten off the horse."

"But I did."

"Yes, you did."

"And the problem would be?"

"I've always been told that any man who stepped foot on the island would disappear. I saw it happen, once," I said.

"Any *man*?" he asked.

"Any man," I repeated.

"No worries. My entire family agrees on only one thing. I am not a man. My stepfather, just before I set out, said, 'If this trip doesn't make a man out of you, nothing will,'" said the stranger.

"How old are you?" I asked.

"Thirteen," the stranger replied.

"Some say thirteen is a man," I said.

"Obviously, the island doesn't agree, as I haven't disappeared," the prince said.

We both laughed. The laughter made him look different to me, almost familiar. And I guess the laughter made me look different to him. Something changed. I, who have been called motormouth and jabber baby and chatty chica, could think of nothing to say. After half a minute all I had thought of was, "Oh. Wow." So that's what I said.

When you're looking at a boy who is cuter than the boys in the magazines, cuter than any boy you've ever dreamed up in your head, a boy who makes you think of Romeo saying lips should be able to touch like hands, a *swoon-provoking* boy, after not seeing *any* boy in real life since you were four, it can be hard to put words together.

I did manage to ask him if he was hungry. He was. And seeing as his royal hotness had interrupted my lunch, I was still hungry too. I started tearing and tossing the greens I had collected. Just to hear his voice I peppered him with questions as I assembled the salad and served it up in a wild lettuce leaf.

I found out he isn't an astronomer like my mother, but he is looking for a star. He is on a mission. I peppered him with more questions. He said he is searching for his kingdom's greatest treasure. He said it's hidden beneath a special star, and he's looking for that star. He said he thinks there is a telescope somewhere on the East Side of the island that will let him see the star. He said he had tied up his boat down at East Island's dock, and that his name is Chance. He said he comes from Raven World. He talked a lot, and fast. But not as fast as my heart was beating.

He comes from Raven World! He knows the place where I was born. He could tell me all about it. I ALMOST SPILLED THE BEANS! Right then and there! Someone my height! My size. My age! I almost shrieked, "I'm from Raven World too!" Except the question after that from him would be, "And why are you here?" And that was a question I couldn't answer without breaking a Big Rule. I just bit the inside of my cheeks and reminded myself of the one truth Mamselle and all three Godmommies always agreed on: I DON'T KNOW WHAT A SPY LOOKS LIKE! ANY-BODY CAN BE A SPY. Usually one of the Godmommies said this about Mamselle but it kinda sorta applies to Chance. I don't know any thirteen-year-old spies, but I don't know any thirteen-year-old anything elses, either. It was a conundrum. But I'm good at conundrums. I needed to know more about this boy without letting him know anything much about me. But most questions tell more about the person asking them than they do about the person answering. How to get around that?

I felt like I was back in the OPT. It was not a good feeling, but it got my brain revved. Something Godmommy Grace always said that had never made sense to me was starting to now: "You can always tell who a person is by what they carry with them on a long, hard journey."

I carried bees and you, Diary, when I came to East Island. That tells a lot about me. G.Mama Dot carried paints, a cast-iron skillet, and a retirement from the bus company plaque, to Bee Isle exile. Godmommy Grace carried a cross, a Bible, and a yoga mat; Godmother Elizabethanne carried a *World Book Encyclopedia*. Mamselle carried a decade's supply of makeup, some very fancy ink and calligraphy pens, and a miniature horse. I knew what I had to ask Chance.

"What's in your saddlebags?"

"That's an odd question."

"I am an odd girl."

"I might like odd girls. Most of the girls I know are ordinary on purpose."

"Ordinary on purpose?"

"They wear the same clothes, just in different colors, they talk the same, they do the same things—ordinary on purpose. Boooring."

"What am I?" I asked.

"Unusual!"

"Unusual?"

"You're wearing a bedsheet, and making salad from stuff you're picking out of the grass . . . good salad, but that's unusual."

"Do you know what's usual on Bee Isle?"

"Is that the name of this place?"

"Yes."

"And what's your name?"

Yikes. My simple question about the saddlebags led to him knowing as much about me as I know about him—exactly what I'd been trying to avoid. But questions are like that. And now my question was going to tell *me* about me. Could I really lie to the very first friend I'd met in a very, very, very long time? Could I lie at first sight? I decided to answer his question with a question. My original question.

"What's in your saddlebags?"

Chance didn't answer me directly. He whistled for his horse, whom he called Ibis. Five times the size of Mamselle's horse, Bayard, Ibis trotted toward us. Chance untied the saddlebag, sat down beside me, then pulled out a chess board, and a black feather, and a tattered copy of *Huckleberry Finn*. A good game, a good book, and an odd feather. This boy was more than hyper-fine. He could be a friend. He could also be a spy. Something seemed fake.

"Where are the chess pieces?" I asked.

"I improvise. Nuts for my opponent. Rocks for me."

"I'll take strawberries."

"You play chess?"

"Yes."

"Most girls don't."

"Every girl on this island does."

"Does that mean you're the only girl on this island?"

"It means I should have said all the girls I know on this island play chess."

"What about the boys?"

145

"There aren't any."

"Until now."

"Until now, chess player."

"Shall we have a game?"

"I thought you were on a mission."

"I haven't had a friend to talk to or play with for weeks. The mission can wait. But finishing lunch can't. What's for dessert?"

After asking this, he didn't even wait for me to get my plate of berries ready before he started eating his. He actually grabbed his plate from me—like I was a serving girl. He's sweet but he's spoiled.

If he hadn't been so rude, or if he had ever slowed down talking, I might have told him that the telescope he was looking for was in my mother's castle tower and how to get there. But he didn't. So I didn't.

We started playing chess and talking. When I was getting the better of him he started tapping his pieces as he played, trying to throw me off. But I didn't fall for that trick. God-mother Elizabethanne had prepared me for it.

I did ask him to tell me more about Raven World. I asked him if he had ever been to Ravencastle. He said yes, but with hesitation in his voice. I tried to get him to tell me about the throne room. I'd always loved the stories the Godmommies told me about it and I wanted to know more. And somehow Chance reminded me of the boy I had played with in the throne room. I peppered him with so many questions he asked me if I was a spy.

Then he asked me how I knew there was a throne room. I said I thought all castles had throne rooms. He said the best and worst hours of his life had happened in Ravencastle's throne room.

What?! I had to know! But was afraid to ask!

Lucky me! Perhaps due to his prior weeks and months of nobody to talk to and the fact that he possibly thought I was some urchin he would never see again, Chance was quite loquacious. I could have called him Chatty Chance. He told me one best time was when he used to play with a friend in the throne room—a special kind of freeze tag— and I almost had a conniption because I just *knew* he was talking about me!

I asked him who the friend was and he said, "Rafael." Rafael? I asked him what was so special about playing freeze tag with Rafael in the throne room, and he said Rafael could perfectly mimic what it looked like to be frozen into a block of ice and, more important, he could pantomime to perfection what some of the souls walking up the stairs to the throne would look like even though they hadn't dared walk. Rafael was rip-roaring funny. I was jealous.

He was my first friend and he didn't even remember me! And he'd made a better friend. While I was stranded on this island with some old ladies. To make matters worse, the next thing he told me was that the Raven King had entrusted him with a secret he wasn't supposed to tell anybody!

"If it's a secret, why are you telling me?"

"You're someone. But you're not anyone in Raven World."

The truth of that statement stung. Guess it served me right by starting the relationship wrong by sending my bees to attack him. I guess sending your bees to attack someone is not the best way, in any world, to begin a friendship.

But I'm in the middle of an ecological crisis. Even if I met a best friend. Even if—I MET A BOY.

I do not have any more time to sit around writing about Chance. Truth.

Rushing back to work,
Black Bee Flummoxed Bright

P.S. The East Side of this island has far more interesting distractions than the West Side. He'd better not meet any of the Princesses without me.

44

Dear Diary,

I bumped into Chance again. Which isn't completely surprising considering the hill I suggested he look for the telescope on, instead of being near the castle tower and my mother's telescope, was right next to the field where I planned on searching, after our lunch, for wild beehives.

I feel a teeny tiny bit guilty for misleading Chance. And great big happy for bumping into him, airs or no airs.

The Godmommies say when you don't know where a thing is, you don't know where a thing isn't. His telescope *could have been* on that hill. But true confession, I knew it probably wasn't. Unless there is a second, hidden-from-me telescope on this island. Not likely.

The Godmommies always say lying to someone is bad, but lying to yourself is worse. I think lying to your diary would be even worse than that, so I am telling you the truth. I wanted Chance to find me, not the telescope. Sorry I'm not sorry.

This time Chance was a lot friendlier; he asked me my name again. This time I told him. B. B. While I searched for wild hives (it was pretty obvious to him pretty soon that there was nothing as big as a telescope anywhere nearby), he starting telling me more about Raven World, like he wanted me to be interested in the place he came from. And he started searching for wild hives too. And after we had found one, working together, we rested over chess and chat.

Chance says Raven World is easy to like. He says it produces the most beautiful flowers in the world and the savory-est herbs and the sweetest spices. He says Raven World is a rich nation with an empty throne, where factions vie for power. That means, basically, that lots of people are fighting to sit where my mama and papa once sat. That most everyone used to consider Raven World a superpower. But Chance says Raven World's power has been diminished and is diminishing more of late because too much of the power is wasted in fights about water rights and mineral rights. He says, when he was little, Raven World was peaceful like Bee Isle. He says Raven World needs a new king and queen sitting atop the Raven thrones to stop all the stabbin' and jabbin' and beefin'.

"What's stabbin' and jabbin' and beefin'?"

"Politics with swords and monarchy."

"Bee Isle is a democracy."

"This place is so pretty I think I might like to live in a democracy."

Chance sounded bashful and modest when he said that, like he didn't want to be too proud of his country. Like he wanted to be respectful of Bee Isle. Then he took my knight.

Then I took his. In two moves, but I took it.

"You're pretty good," he said.

What a change. When he was eating that salad, sometimes he sounded so spoiled, imperious, and high and mighty, he reminded me of the Queens!

I'm thinking maybe that's just the way he acts when he first meets people, like Jane Austen's (or really Lizzie Bennet's) Mr. Darcy. By the time he was telling me the country he worked for was really cool, I was thinking, *probably not as cool as you.*

My mind is dancing like my bees were dancing in West Island just before we made this trip—in dizzy patterns that don't work!

Chance asked me to tell him my real name, not my nickname, but I ignored his question. Chance doesn't seem to like being ignored. He says there are other princes he knows that I might like to meet. Princes I might more readily tell my real name to.

He doesn't think I like him. Is it bad that I think that's sort of cool, Diary? I think Princess Rubydarling would make him a little jealous. Play hard to get. I want to poke him a bit, but it's hard, maybe impossible, right now, this moment—the day I met the first boy I've spoken to since I started all these *changes*—to even *imagine* trying not to show I like him back, when he's starting to act, a little, like he's starting to like me. What was it Juliet said? "I should have been more strange."

Except Chance doesn't exactly feel like my boyfriend; he feels like my friend who is a boy, like the very best friendboy in the world, and I want him to know everything about me. I don't want him to run after me and I don't want to run after him. I want to run together.

Just as I was thinking this I saw a girl that looked exactly like what I think Ruby looks like and she had a ruby around her neck and she was shaking her head no and smiling, then she blew me kisses and spirited off into wherever, leaving me to wonder, "Was that a meeting?" Who knows. But I did know something, and I said it.

I said I don't want to meet another prince. He said my pareo was pretty, that he'd never seen anything that looked so cool—in both senses of the word. When he said that, my face got all warm. He said I've read more books than anybody he's ever met, and he said it like it's a good thing. I told him there's not that much else to do on an island. He laughed, and when it died down, I asked him if he knows a lot of girls. He said he does. I told him all the boys I know are characters in books. We both laughed at that. We like a lot of the same books. And we have the same three favorite poets: Langston Hughes, Gwendolyn Brooks, and Will Shakespeare.

I want to know what novels Chance likes to read but I'm afraid to ask. I don't want to hate the books Chance likes. Chance asked me again to tell him my name. Again I didn't. Boy, is Big Rule Three cramping my style. Anyway, Chance started talking, again, about some of his prince friends back home. Snoo-ooze!

I am FALLING IN LOVE with Chance—even though it seems like Chance wants me to fall in love with some other boy or prince because he's afraid I don't like him and he doesn't want to like me if I don't like him! Even though I think he might make the very best friendboy I never imagined. Boys are confusing.

I want to go with Chance to Raven World and get unconfused!

Maybe the Princesses will come out and I will meet them, really quickly, today, now, in time for me to leave the island with Chance. Or maybe these flickering glimpses count? But I don't think they do. And I can't imagine anyone else in all of Raven World or The Other World being even half as cute as Chance—who has now started talking about other princesses he wants me to meet back in Raven World, which is a lot worse than hearing him talk about his prince friends he wants me to meet.

The only princesses I want to meet are supposed to be on this side of the island. And I believe they are. Now that I've caught what had to be a glimpse of Rubydarling I feel more sure that the other seven Princesses are here, with me, on the island, dashing around, so quick I can't exactly see them but I can feel them and I can almost see them. And that's a kind of meeting. Just out of the corner of my eye.

I wanted Chance to get on about his business so I could get on about mine. And even if he didn't get on about his business I planned to get on about mine, anyway.

I will not be too busy with my bee chores and Chance to meet the Princesses. I don't want to be stuck on this island for the rest of my life. I want to bring democracy to Ravencastle! I don't have to be its queen; I could be its president. Or not. But maybe if I want to be a president I should move to The Other World. All I know for sure is none of that is happening if I don't meet The Eight Princesses, since even if I pass my OPT, I can't make my way off the island without them, thanks to Big Rule Number Two . For the first time in my life, I have a plan. An exciting plan—me, President of Ravencastle.

Sitting across the chess board from Chance and dreaming of my presidency, I closed my eyes and hugged myself. Then it felt like someone was hugging me. I wondered if Chance had gone crazy and suddenly taken a leap of faith, throwing his arms around me. I opened my eyes. He was still sitting on the other side of the chess board and I knew in my heart it was Pearl who had just hugged me. But how?

I was so distracted daydreaming. Chance won the game. Unlike me had less than zero interest in completing the task at hand. I told him he had to. I told him I don't want to be friends with a boy who doesn't do what he sets out to do. And I want to be best friends with him. I said it was time to get down to business.

I told him I thought the telescope he was looking for was in the castle's tower. I told him how to find his way to the path through the thicket and the meadows to Tower Castle.

Since I first saw Chance standing on the island, dancing around that Big Rule Number Two, the island has gotten a whole lot more interesting.

Love, love, love!
BeeBee

45

Dear Diary,

Doing the right thing can be too too sweet! Last hive check of the day I tasted a drop of East Island honey and I saw beads of fresh, clean, sticky, bright-burning wax.

The Apies Candle Company survives! Yes! I will be able to buy so many new heifers for the heifer project and a microscope for a new clinic in Soweto. And I'm going to start crowd-source funding! Yes! And so, so many other things! Apies philanthropies will thrive. My West Island queen bees are very, very popular with the East Island worker bees.

East Island rocks! Whole hives are joining our new apiary. I hope maybe somehow, someway, the bees understand working for BeeBee's Apiary means working for peace, and for the joy of fresh starts.

It should be time to rest and be thankful—if I didn't have so much to do and tell!

After the last hive check I hiked over to Deep Pond to make camp for the night and relax a little by swimming beneath the moon.

Chance was off on Ibis to check out the telescope. He didn't think we should be in the castle alone at night together. I told him I would camp out at Deep Pond and he could have the castle to himself for as long as he needed. He said he didn't know if that would be an hour or a night but once he had found what he needed to find or decided he couldn't find it, he was headed to West Island to check for other telescopes. I told that boy they weren't there, but he said he was bound to see for himself—the Godmommies always said boys were hard-headed. At least the great telescope hunt would keep him on the island a little longer. Then he would come back to East Island and leave from the dock.

I was floating on my back, moon bathing, looking at the stars, talking to my favorite constellations, telling them all about Chance, when he came back, at a full gallop, on Ibis!

He had crossed paths with the giant bear. And that embarrassed Chance (so he later told me), because he hadn't believed the Great Pale Bear existed. He told me that when we were paddling in Deep Pond. I told him that once you'd seen it, you were allowed to call it the GBP. But I'm getting ahead of myself.

But paddling in Deep Pond with Chance was so sweet I can't help but get ahead of myself!

When he told the story (as we paddled!) he said he couldn't decide if it was when he saw GPB, or when he heard GPB's stomach growling, or when he smelled the stink of GPB's scat, or when he smelled the stink of GPB's breath—but somewhere in the middle of his total GPB experience,

Chance started thinking about me alone, surrounded by bees and honey, of me as bear bait.

I think he came back because he wanted to see me again. I may only know one boy—but even the newest ingénue can figure out that if a boy comes back twice, he wants to see you. No matter what excuse he gives.

Flashback. When Chance arrived at Deep Pond on Ibis, I almost drowned myself! A swimming pareo is not the easiest thing in the world to swim in. It's long. So long it goes down to your feet. When I saw Chance I got so excited I almost tangled my feet in the hem.

He tied his horse up to a tree, dashed behind a rock, then reappeared in orange shorts with purple polka dots that he insisted were swimming trunks. Silly trunks more like. Then he jumped into the water.

Watching him cannonball I almost forgot how to swim! He looked that beautiful. And that foolish, all at once! He started swimming toward me. I splashed him away.

I was pretty sure if he got too close my bees would start stinging him—and me. They *are* guard bees. And the reach of the Godmommies *is* long. And I could see him better from a little bit of distance as he swam in wide laps around me. And a fine view of a new friend's smile is not a good thing—it's a great thing.

We talked about everything. Constellations. Huckleberry Finn. Chess strategy. Even godmothers! Then he said he wanted to know who my people were. I told him it was "none of his beeswax." We both laughed. Then he said "zip" and I said "zap" and neither of us knew why. It was just funny.

I wanted to tell him who my father was, but I knew swimming with a mysterious boy in a pond, with the sky all full of purple and red, is no place to break one of The Three Big Rules.

I think Chance is not just any prince. I think—*I suspect*—Chance is my old friend Enchantment, who didn't use to be a prince at all but who must be one now. Can that be?

"Do you know what the OPT is?" I asked.

"Of course, I just passed it."

"You passed the OPT?"

"Barely, but yes!"

"The Official Princess Test?"

"The Official *Prince* Test!"

"I didn't know there was one for boys."

"I didn't know there was one for girls."

Now we both knew. And we knew he had passed and I was waiting. Chance asked me all about my test. He said he loved my answers.

This would be the most exciting day of my life; or the most dangerous day, or the saddest day—depending on whether or not Chance really were Enchantment!

He said I looked like a fairy princess. He said I looked familiar. When he said that I wanted to tell him the whole truth. Rule Three Rule Three Rule Three. A moonlight pond swim is no time to break a Big Rule.

He has skin the color of caramel. It's not smooth

158

everywhere, but his face is rough from the wind, rough and beautiful. And his hands are rough too, probably from pulling Ibis's reins, and the ropes to shift the sails of his boat, too. When he reached out to splash me, just as I dove beneath the water and swam further away from him, his hand brushed my foot. His roughness is sweeter than softness.

And Chance has the deepest brown eyes. And they're not just pretty and beautiful, they are fireworks and birthday candles, they are now and fun, and love and forever. I LOVE CHANCE. I love having a best friend.

He said he thinks his stepfather sent him searching for a lost star not so that he would find it, but so that he would get killed. He said that his stepfather doesn't really like him. He said his stepfather, the duke, wants to be king but he's afraid to sit on the Raven Throne—because he knows he's not really supposed to be the king and fears he'll get frozen. This is when I lost my breath. Chance *was* really Enchantment. *But he did not recognize me!*

Maybe he wasn't Enchantment. Or maybe I'd just changed so much he didn't see who I used to be—his friend. I thought of the story about the time when I was really little, and my friend Enchantment and I saw my cousins getting frozen into giant blocks of ice, and it was almost not a story. It was almost a memory. I squinted again to make sure Chance was Enchantment. I thought he was. But the last time I saw him I was four. I wasn't sure. I didn't want to break the rule and tell him who I am. Even if I said my full real name, I wasn't sure he would be willing to believe this wild island beekeeper with calloused feet was once the silk-shod daughter of the Raven King.

I didn't tell him my name. Instead I told him that *if* (big if!) I passed the Princess Test, one day I would be the Queen of Bee Isle and I would need powerful allies. I asked him if our countries could be friends.

I said that Bee Isle made a wonderful home for artists and astronomers and just like Ireland we're not going to tax writers. Chance interrupted.

He said after I became Queen of Bee Isle he would come and marry me and together we would figure out a way to put Ravencastle back on the right path. Hold on. HOLD ON. MARRY ME?!? Did he just say that?!? He was just teasing me, but I was amused. We plotted how we could sit on the Raven Thrones together. I asked him if his stepfather the duke was very courageous. Chance said that he was not. I told Chance that it might be smart, upon his return, to start regaling his stepfather with tales of people who tried for the crown but were frozen into blocks of ice. I told him that sometimes it's wiser to trust in people's weaknesses than it is to trust in their strengths. Chance was amazed.

"How did you figure that out?"

"I read *The Prince* as part of my OPT prep."

"What's *The Prince*?"

"It's this book that tells you all about how to be powerful."

"Machabelly?"

I laughed. And Chance laughed with me. The water rippled with our laughter.

Then for the first time but not, I hope, for the last time I, Black Bee Bright, gazed face to face, eye to eye, into Valentine love.

"I see stars in your eyes," said Chance.

"In my eyes?" I asked, laughing at his silliness.

"You're pretty," he said, sounding serious, very serious.

I wanted to swoon. When he said, "I'm tired of looking for the darkstar, I won't search for the darkstar any longer," I almost actually did swoon. I barely heard him when he whispered, "I seek nothing but what I have found."

"What did you just call the star?" I asked, sidetracked.

"The darkstar," Chance replied.

"That's what the Godmommies call the stone in my necklace," I said. I turned the chain around so the gems were showing. I pointed to the star. Chance looked stunned. He paddled closer to me. "That stone came from the hilt of the Raven King's sword. He showed me the gaping hole the day he died. He told me, the day he died, that when I saw that stone again it would be with the one who should sit on his throne," said Chance.

"You spoke to the Raven King?" I asked.

"That's why I came to this island."

"What did he say to you?"

"He said his daughter was hidden in the Delphinious

161

Quadrant and when I turned thirteen I should go and find her."

"How can you remember that? Weren't you four when he died?"

"I was six. The war started when I was four and the Raven King went into hiding when I was four, but he didn't die till I was six. We were in hiding."

"Who are 'we'?" I asked.

"The king, the queen, and I," said Chance.

"You knew them when you were . . . six?"

"My parents got killed in the war. The Raven King took care of me."

"The queen too?"

"The queen too. If that is the darkstar, what is beneath it is our kingdom's greatest treasure."

"My heart's beneath it."

"Then you must be the Raven King's daughter."

I couldn't say yes. So I said what I could say: "Zip." And he said what spoke volumes: "Zap." Then I said "zip" again. It felt too good not to.

"Black Bee Bright, Princess of Light," said Chance, questioning and acclaiming with the same breath.

"B. B., wild girl of Bee Isle," I said.

"My first friend."

"My first friend."

So Chance is Enchantment. We hugged and the bees did not sting us. We hugged and we cried for the parents we had lost and we each cried for the friend we had just found.

It was all tear-provoking. Everything had changed. We got out of the water and sat on the bank.

"I have to go," said Chance.

"Now?"

"Absolutely. My uncle checks up on me. His men might follow me. If I stay here I will lead them to you. I must keep going, and . . ."

"And?"

"I have something for you from the saddlebag." Chance whistled, and Ibis trotted up to where we were sitting. Chance poked into his saddlebag again. He took out the feather I had seen before.

"You showed me this already."

"Showed, but didn't tell."

"So tell."

"On the day he died the Raven King gave me this feather and made me promise I would give it to you and make you promise to return to Raven World. This feather will fly you back. It is from your father's crown."

"I'm BeeBee," I said.

"BeeBee?" he repeated.

"President of Apies Candles. Chairperson of Philanthropy. Maybe soon to be ruler of an isolated island," I said.

In the dark, by the water, was (as I kept reminding myself) NO time to break a big rule. But Chance had so many questions!

"If you're not the Raven King's daughter, who are your people?" asked Chance.

"The Godmommies and Mamselle," I said.

"Go back to them. You're not old enough to be out here alone with wild bears," said Chance.

"I handled the bear. And you're not in charge of me. I have a few more things I need to do before I leave this side of the island. You're not the only one here on some special fancy mission. *You* can wait for *me*. If you want," I said.

"Can't. You might not be able to tell me you are Black Bee Bright. I know you are Black Bee Bright and I know that my very presence on this island puts you in danger. You should take the feather, I should get on my boat tonight, and we must hope to one day meet in Ravencastle."

I wanted to kiss Chance's cheek. So I did. Because he was my old friend and because he was going away. Because kissing him on the cheek was nicer than crying. Then I stared into Chance's eyes for half a second. Amazed as I was by his words, I was more amazed by the sight of the stars in my eyes dancing in his eyes. I wondered if he could see the stars in his eyes dancing in mine. Then he . . . almost kissed me! Then he didn't. He kissed his finger and planted the kiss on my nose.

"Our first kiss should be in Ravencastle."

"If we have a first kiss," I said.

We made a plan. He's going by boat. I'm going by Ibis. He's leaving me his horse and the feather. We will meet in Ravencastle in a year and day. If not before.

I wish I had met The Eight Princesses by now. If I had met The Eight Princesses I would follow Chance off this island. Right now.

I want to ask Chance to tell me more about the Raven King. But I don't. I don't trust myself to keep my silences if he starts talking about my papa.

We traveled back fast to his boat. I rode Ibis; Chance trotted beside us. Too soon we were back at the East Island dock. All the while we travelled, he talked about getting back to Raven World and finding allies for me. And he made me promise over and over that I would use the feather to return in a year and a day.

Now he's tinkering on the boat with the rigging of his sails and I'm sitting on the shore writing in you.

Besotted to be watching Chance struggle with the sails and ropes,
Black Bee, swoon, swoon Bright

46

Dear Diary,

Chance just left. And I have returned to Castle Tower. I wonder if meeting one prince is equal to meeting Eight Princesses. I don't think so. I'm full of missing. I miss Chance and I miss my Godmommies and I miss my mother and my father. I'm even jealous Chance has memories of my father. I don't remember my father. I know stories about him but that's not the same thing. I remember my mother. I remember how close we came to the stars when we flew here. It's all wonderful and it's all too much.

I LOVE CHANCE AND I HOPE HOPE HOPE CHANCE LOVES ME. I scribble that in the dust on my mother's dresser. I like the way those words sound. I want him to be my best friend. The island has gotten so much bigger and more interesting since I saw Chance standing in my new bee field.

How can places you have known become bigger and more interesting in a single afternoon? Chance can arrive.

Chance, I hope Enchantment, can arrive. Enchantment can arrive. I feel like Miranda when she first met Ferdinand. Exactly like Miranda. I am on an island in the middle of nowhere and someone unexpected has arrived, someone who makes me wonder about brave new worlds, with such princes in them.

I've saved my bees and fallen in love all in the same day.

Black Bee Bright,
The Raven Queen's daughter

47

Dear Diary,

I can't fall asleep. Chance has moved things around too much for me to sleep. Or maybe it's just that Chance has been here keeping me awake. Or maybe I just don't like things out of place. He pulled up a chair near the telescope. He left orange peels on the telescope ledge. And there are dusty boy-footprints across the floor. I get up and tidy up. It is different knowing that Chance has been here. I sit down at my mother's vanity table to look in the mirror and see if I look any different and am alarmed to see the silly sentence I scribbled in the dust and blush to think Chance might have read it—if I had written it a day earlier. Clearly Chance had sat at my mother's vanity. There's a blackberry-stained fingerprint on my mother's crown. I pick it up in my hands. I polish away the print. I polish back the shine.

I am alone again in the tower but I am not lonely. I feel my mother's presence. I wonder if that means she has made her way to heaven. Atop each point on my mother's crown is a star. I wonder if I pass the OPT whether they will put bees on the tips of my crown—or fireflies—or both. I take my mother's crown into bed with me. In the firefly light I see the names of all the Princesses engraved inside and my mother's name.

Tomorrow I will do nothing but look for the Princesses.

Drowsy Wow-sy Beebee

48

Dear, dear Diary,

Everything has changed again. Just before dawn. All Eight Princesses in a single room. I had awoken early. The crown wasn't on my head; my right hand was clutched 'round it. I didn't want to go back to sleep, so instead I decided to draw pictures as a present for the Godmommies. I began to plan for my return—thinking maybe the Princesses had decided to visit West Island at exactly the same time I'd decided to visit East. It seemed possible because the Princesses are a lot like me.

I didn't like facing return to the other side of the island as a failure—but I was ready to return to the Godmommies— one way or another. I had saved my bees. I had met Chance. And I had heard from my parents. Too much had happened for me not to go back and tell the Godmommies. If I had to make a second trip to the East Side of the island to find the Princesses, I would make a second trip. Enough was enough. So I started drawing.

In the early morning I heard a tune, *be-da-be-da-be-la-la,* that I hadn't heard in a very, very long time.

A nightbird was tweeting the song my daddy whistled back in Ravencastle. *Be-da-be-da-be-la-la.*

I followed nightbird's *be-da-be-da-be-la-la* into a waking dream. The early morning wind blew and on it was the scent of my mother. In the half-dream time of almost-day, I sorted through all that had happened to figure out and draw what was most important. Me in Mama's mirror all fancy dressed. My devouring Mama's Shakespeare library and bird texts. Me tending the birds. Me praying for Mama. Me plotting with Chance to take our places atop the Raven Thrones. Me walking alone across the desert—with only Rotty and Zuzu trotting beside me. Me all-over shivery with the pleasure of the wind hugging me and perfuming me and making the flowers dance before my eyes. Me painting the picture of me on the rock. Me wearing a crown with a darkstar right in the middle and golden bees on its tips. I made sketches of all of that—then I went back to sleep beneath my picture quilt.

I awoke and I knew—all Eight Princesses are me! I am Rubydarling and Sass and Gigi, and Ammie and Pearl and Jaz and Tope and ChaCha. I looked down at my magic quilt, and where the symbols had been were now pictures of me.

The heart was replaced with a picture of me in Mama's mirror all fancy dressed. The simple book was replaced with a picture of me in Mama's library. The circle with a baby in it was replaced with me tending my baby birds. The infinity symbol was replaced by me praying for Mama.

171

Randall and Randall Williams

The crown was replaced with a picture of me and Chance plotting to take our places in Ravencastle. The leaf was replaced by a picture of me walking alone across the desert. The rainbow palm was replaced by a picture of me shivering in pleasure from the wind's touch and scent; the paintbrush was replaced by my Me-on-the-Rock painting. Where the nine-pointed black star had been was an amazing portrait of me, B. B. The new me I know to be a girl who loves being pretty, and praying, and taking care,

and studying, and power, and walking about in nature, and the pleasure of her senses, and creating beauty. All The Eight Princesses are me!

And I knew just how to tell the Godmommies.

Exuberatingly,
B. B., who will be returning to Ravencastle—because she has the power of eight princesses inside of her and her very own plans.

But first I'm returning to West Island. My plans include telling the Godmommies and Mamselle all!

49

Dear Diary,

Packing for return. I came with only a rucksack and a pole to tote my hives, I will return with a rucksack and very full saddlebags . . . there are so many things I want to take back with me. My mother's crown is in my rucksack. Her tambourine is in it, too. My father's feather is braided into my hair. I am on my way back to the Godmommies!!!!! Triumphant!!!!!!

Older and Exhilarated,
Black Bee

50

Dear Diary,

I knew just how I wanted to spill the beans! I knocked
on the door and the Godmommies opened it wide
and started hugging and kissing and hooping and
hollerin'. I pulled away and started running and
screaming and they ran and screamed after me. I ran
straight towards Mamselle's door but she heard the
commotion before we got there and she came out
shouting and screaming too. I gave her a hug, then
pulled away from her and ran to the beach—and into
the water.

    I did not disappear. I floated. And the Godmom-
mies and Mamselle rushed into the water, too, hooping and hollering even louder than before. Rotty was
so shocked by our behavior he barked on the shore and
wouldn't come in. He had never seen one of us swim in
the ocean. Zuzu, who had swum with my mother, ran
right into the surf and swam into my arms.

The Diary of B. B. Bright, Possible Princess

I have stepped off the island and didn't disappear!
I have seen The Eight Princesses! The Godmommies
are overjoyed.

Buzzing Bright,
B. B.

51

Dear Diary,

They made me welcome-home apple crepes. It was the first time I'd had hot food in weeks. When I smelled the butter bubbling in the skillet I started to cry. Happy tears. Tired tears. Sad-about-Mama tears. Sad-Chance-is-gone tears. And just a few I-may-never-see-him-again tears.

I wanted to tell them all about bees, and boys, and ball-gowns, and bears, but all I could do was sniffle, and smile, and gobble down the best crepes I had ever tasted while the God-mommies and Mamselle sniffled and smiled too. Meeting eight princesses and a prince is tuckering. Returning home and figuring out how to talk about it is even more tuckering.

It's the middle of the day and I need a nap—but naps remind me of the quilt and I have to show the Godmom-mies the quilt. I start pulling it little by little out of the rucksack—they do not seem surprised, they seem pleased—until they see the picture of me and Chance plotting.

"Whoa, no!" said G.Mama Dot.

"One of The Eight Princesses was a Prince?" asked Godmother Elizabethanne.

"It looks like you have a lot a lot to tell us," said God-mommy Grace.

No bees got tended that day. We sat and drank cups of lime leaf tea and nibbled on spoons of peanut butter and honey and talked and talked until the story of my time on the East Side of the island was fully told and the moon was high and bright.

Slipping beneath my story quilt, I finally understood what the Godmommies meant when they said the quilt predicted the future. The quilt they sewed for me predicts every girl's future—if she is lucky enough to be all she was born to be—and I think they left some patches blank—so I could be some new things nobody could imagine or be but me.

Exhausted But Proud,
B. B.

52

Dear Diary,

The Godmommies let me drink coffee today! It had lots of milk in it but it was coffee. They want me to stay up all day so I can get back on a proper schedule. They say if I'm old enough to go to East Island and meet a boy I'm old enough to drink coffee.

After coffee we sat down to a meal of quiche and pumpkin soup and the Godmommies and Mamselle firing away at me with questions.

They couldn't wait to hear even more about what had happened on the other side of the island. They wanted to see the feather again. They wanted to see the crown. They wanted to know every word Chance had said. We talked all afternoon. We talked through dinner. Before long we were cozy in my room and all three of the Godmommies were tucked up on my bed, and Mamselle was in my old rocking chair, and they were still listening and I was still talking.

Even Mamselle laughed when I told the story of crazy me and the GPB. And I was so pleased with myself. Then they asked the big question. They asked me what it was like to meet the Princesses.

I had only one word for the experience. Octagonal.

It was a word I'd made up riding back across the desert. It meant holy, and creative, and powerful, and nurturing, and beautiful, and independent, and sensate, and intellectual all tied up into one happy girl. Octagonal.

The Godmommies got it. Mamselle got it. A moment after I said the word, they echoed it back to me.

Octagonal,
B. B.

53

Dear Diary,

A week after I got back, more of my West Island bees swarmed and followed my scouts to East Island and my new hives. Though I had Ibis to ride and that shortened the distances, between racing back and forth to lead swarms and establish new hives and telling my East Island tale, I didn't have time to write. And, true confession, the little time I did have to write, I spent writing letters to Chance! I write and twirl the feather in my hair.

Apologetically,
BeeBee

P.S. I haven't sent any of my scribbles to Chance yet. It will take him months to get to Ravencastle and I don't know where to send a letter to a sailor looking for a star in the wrong sky. But I'm going to figure it out!

54

Dear Diary,

IT CAME! The letter. My OPT results.

I ripped open the envelope. Before I could read the results of the Official Princess Test for myself, Mamselle cleared her throat, then pronounced, "Black Bee Bright declared Princess of Light."

"I passed?"

"You passed. With flying colors."

I liked that—flying colors. I fingered the feather braided into my hair.

"Do you think it is time for you to return to Ravencastle, Black Bee Bright, Princess of Light?" asked Mamselle.

"In about a year minus a few days."

There were all the books in my mother's library that I still had to read. There were the chess moves I had to learn from Godmother Elizabethanne and the painting lessons I wanted to take with G. Mama Dot and the rest of the sun salute I still had to learn from Godmommy Grace. There was getting to do something else with Mamselle instead of prepare for the OPT. There was packing up Apies Candle Company. There was migrating more bees to the East Side of the island. There was wearing my beautiful necklace on the island where I saw The Eight Princesses. But tonight it was enough to swim again in the ocean with Rotty, to step off the island and not disappear—to know the best time is now and the best place is here—and in 363 days I will be in Ravencastle.

I'm going home!!!!!!!!!!!

The one and only Black Bee Bright,
Princess of Light for Real

The End

Vocabulary Notes

Here are some pages for you to write down any words you don't know that you read in my diary—and their definitions, which you can find in a dictionary. If you want, you can also make up a sentence with each word in it. I don't think I should have all the fun of writing in this book to myself!

B. B.